BENEATH THE HILL

by the same author

DOWN FROM THE LONELY MOUNTAIN: *California Indian Tales*

Beneath the Hill

Jane Louise Curry

Illustrated by Imero Gobbato

Harcourt, Brace & World, Inc., New York

First edition

Library of Congress Catalog Card Number: AC 67-10202

Printed in the United States of America

For my mother and father
and Mary An and Bill

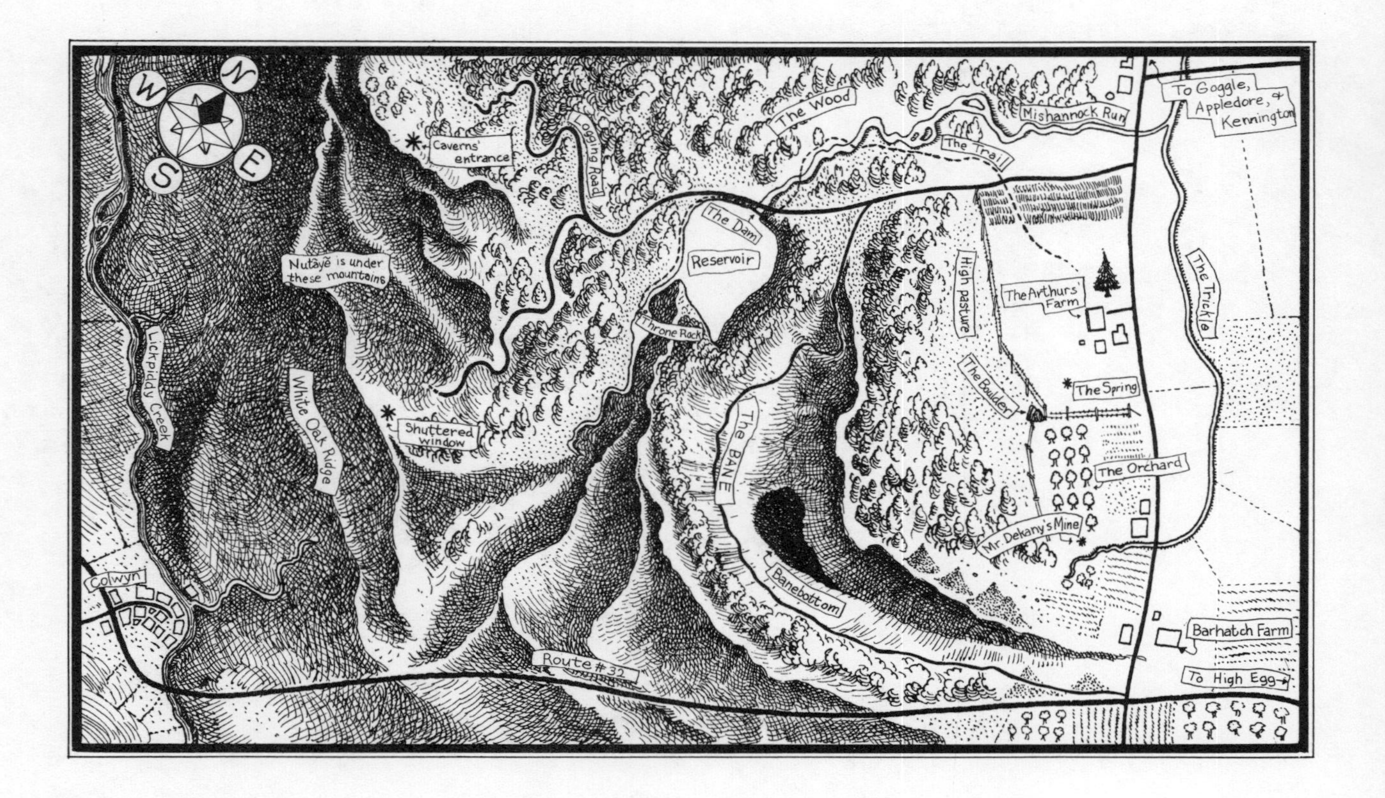
N
W
E
S
Caverns' entrance
Logging Road
The Wood
Mishannock Run
To Goggle, Appledore, & Kennington
The Trail
The Dam
Reservoir
Nutáyé is under these mountains
The Arthurs' Farm
High pasture
The Trickle
Throne Rock
Lickpiddy Creek
White Oak Ridge
The Boulder
The Spring
Shuttered window
The BANE
The Orchard
Mr. Dekany's Mine
Colwyn
Banebottom
Barhatch Farm
Route #32
To High Egg

Chapter One

Miggle wriggled deep into the dip in the middle of the old feather bed and pulled her pillow tightly over her head to shut out the noise of the Elephants. She had not had a moment to herself all afternoon or evening when she could laugh out loud, though she had been near to bursting with smugness and delight at her own cleverness. Now she giggled into the mothball-and-lavender fragrance of the feather bed and then raised up to punch the pillow back into shape. If you put it over your head, you couldn't breathe; and if you didn't, you could hear the Elephants high on the ridge all night long, or at least until you got tired of noticing them and fell off to sleep. But Miggle had the new game to think of, and she wasn't the least bit sleepy. She stretched out on her back and made a tent from the sheet by covering her head and sticking up her knees. Arthur Arthur thought he was so smart! He wasn't the only one who could invent games and lead expeditions and charm everyone into believing that everything he said was so. So old

Miggle was just a dumb old girl? Well, the bait was set, and all she had to do was remember to keep quiet and not be bossy, even if she was the oldest by five weeks.

She peered out from under the sheet. In the big double bed her sister Trish and red-haired Kit were already still. The house was quiet. Miggle closed her eyes and breathed very carefully so as not to make a sound. After a bit, noises too small to be noticed in the daytime separated from each other, sharpened, and carried clearly to her ears. There was a squirrel or chipmunk up on the roof; a mosquito hovered by the window; and through the wall that divided her room from the loft room that was Trish's when there wasn't company, she heard a faint buzz. Arthur and Stevie were still awake and whispering. Well, they hadn't seen each other for a long time. Not since Christmas. Just so they weren't planning to go off fishing or something tomorrow and leave her with the younger girls. The corn in the field opposite the house rustled in a faint breeze. Miggle began to count off on her fingers the steps of tomorrow's game. It had taken a week for the planning, and she hadn't gotten the last piece, the carven walnut-shaped box, hidden in the Wood until this morning, only an hour before Mr. and Mrs. Arthur bundled her and Trish and Rover into the car to go to meet the cousins' bus in High Egg village. This summer the cousins were going to stay for a whole month.

Rover—whose real name was Morton—was Miggle's two-year-old brother. He had lost interest in the cousins when he heard they weren't bringing their dogs with them; but Trish, who was eight, had been bouncing up and down for days. This morning she had been up early dusting window sills, tying frilly bows on the cats and dogs, and making a display on her bedspread of ribbons, pins, doll clothes, and the tiny antique mother-of-pearl comb—all the treasures new since Kit, also eight, had visited the farm at Christmas. All the Griffiths had come that time: Uncle Steve, Aunt Jill (who was Mrs. Arthur's sister), Stevie, Kit, and the baby, who slept all of the time. Mr. Griffith was Mr. Arthur's first cousin, which meant that Miggle, Stevie, Trish, and Kit—as well as Rover and the baby—were not only first cousins, but first cousins once removed—or was it second cousins? But explaining this to their friends involved drawing diagrams that never seemed to make things clear.

There had been more family at Christmastime as well: Uncle Tim, Mr. Arthur's brother, had driven all the way from Ohio in a snowstorm with Aunt Kate and Dub—which was what all of the cousins called Arthur Arthur. It was short for "Double"—because of his double-barreled name. He liked it. He would have hated being "Artie."

Actually, Dub liked almost anything, from frogs' eggs and nasty beetles to the stories and pictures in the ancient *Victor Book of the Opera*, where Siegfried and Wotan bulged like TV wrestlers and Elsa was as fat as Mrs. Dekany next door. Dub didn't care much for collections, though. If Miggle and Stevie bargained over foreign postage stamps or matchbook-cover swaps, he snorted and said that since they hadn't been to the places themselves, so that the stamps or matchbooks were real reminders, what was the point? Oh, rocks were interesting, even pretty; but they were prettier on the ground than in a shoebox. Coins were all right. You might go to

Ireland one day, and an Irish penny or shilling would come in handy. Besides, the harp design was nice, which was more than could be said for most of the stamps. Dub was very positive.

Miggle frowned into the darkness, remembering the fate of her terrarium. Last summer at Girl Scout camp she had made this really nice one out of a peach crate about five inches deep, an old enameled basin, and some window screening. You put the basin in and filled all around it with good rich dirt. Then you planted moss and little ferns and wildflowers in the dirt, so that the moss covered the edges of the basin like grass on the banks of a pond. Then you filled up the pond with water out of the creek. Miggle had taken some of the nicest of the new stones gathered for her rock collection and set them around the terrarium very artistically, with one very large piece of quartz sparkling up out of the middle of the pond. Before tacking the wire-screen roof on, she had put in some tadpoles, a middling-sized garter snake, and some real interesting moths with feelers like big feathery fans. When she had brought it home, Mrs. Arthur ruled that it had to stay out on the sun porch and that Miggle had to make a door in its screen roof and put in live flies or gnats or something every day for the snake. That wasn't much fun. Still, the moss and flowers grew and the tadpoles lost their tails. But by August the moths had disappeared, and the snake hid under the rocks most of the time.

Then Dub and Stevie and Kit had come for a week, and Dub up and asked, "Why?"

"What a silly question," said Miggle. "So I can watch 'em, of course."

Dub had said "Why?" to that, too.

"Don't be such a nit! So I can learn about them," she remembered answering with a lofty air. And then old Double-Arthur had picked up the terrarium, kicked open the screen door on the porch, and marched out, with the four others at his heels. They went through the gate and down the road past the Dekanys' to the spot where the Trickle made a quiet little pond before it slipped into the culvert and slid under the road. Dub set the terrarium down at the water's edge, took out his pocket knife, pried the screening loose, and then moved back to sit down on the grass. Miggle had been furious. She sputtered and would have cried, but Dub gave her one of those "dumb old girl" looks and said, "Watch!" and so she had watched in spite of herself.

The delicate, nervous motion of the little snake as it raised its head and flickered its tongue and the frozen pose of each of the small frogs among the moss held the children suspended in a sudden awareness that at last movement for these creatures could have real purpose, that it had none before, and that for some unclear reason snakes and frogs were . . . important. The choice of freedom, after five minutes of paralysis, was made by the snake in one smooth glide down and out of sight into the grass—and by the frogs in five erratic hops into the Trickle. It was cheered by the children with three rousing "hip-hip-hurrahs!" and celebrated with a race to answer the lunch bell. Arthur had been right. Arthur was *always* right. Miggle hadn't figured out why, but things always seemed to turn out that way. He led them in "real" games, as he put it, and scoffed at Miggle's "silly girls" games. He said they were only busy games made to fill up time. Miggle, naturally, always grumbled and said that everything he liked was "real" only because he liked it. What was so real about saying that the crab-apple thickets beyond the lower meadow were the thorny barrier to the Wood of Broceliande and that the welling springs beyond were the border of the land where the other Arthur rides and where the Green Knight's castle lies hidden? Miggle was convinced that "real" meant nothing but that old Dub was determined to like his own ideas better than anybody else's. Anyway—she had rescued the terrarium and painted the outside of the box white; and it made a very good planter. She had saved up her allowances and bought a miniature pine tree—a Japanese bonsai—all twisted and artistic-looking, and after a winter indoors the planter looked better than ever.

But *this* time was going to be different. Arthur was going to stumble upon an adventure, and they *would* have fun. When they had all admitted as much, Miggle just *might* tell them she had planned it. Still, it would be fun to keep that a secret for a while, and the longer the adventure lasted, the better. One time when the orchard had been Sherwood Forest and the side lawn the Nottingham tournament field, they had spun out a whole week's worth of adventures. Dub and Stevie had even put a plank across Mishannock Run and had a whacking good battle with quarterstaves in the middle, and they didn't mind a bit getting wet and floundering around in the cold water.

Miggle smiled under the sheet. This morning she had hidden the third clue far up Mishannock Run under the Throne Rock, where you could sit in midstream just above the little falls and fish in the calm pool at your feet. It was, like the other clues, scratched in old-fashioned letters—with ſ instead of *s*—on one of the squares of thin copper she had bought from the remnants box at the Hobby World shop in Kennington. She had filed and hammered the edges to look worn, blackened the metal in a candle flame, and then wrapped each piece in a square of fragile old silk from the attic scrap bag. The best touch, she thought, had been to cover each packet with red candle wax—it had taken a long time to drip it properly—and then to press in good sooty dirt all over the wax.

The clues were all hidden in good places, places that would have been much the same over a hundred years ago when Nathan Ample had cleared the land and built the farmhouse in which the Arthurs lived. Miggle wasn't sure that the tree she had climbed to find a hole for the mysterious treasure would have been big enough in 1830 or so to *hide* a treasure in, but then everything else would be perfectly convincing, so nobody would notice. Everybody would be puzzling over the treasure, not the tree. Miggle let out a happy snort and turned over under the sheet with a bounce that made the springs creak horribly.

"What's so funny?" Trish hissed, unexpectedly awake. "Nobody can sleep with those old cranes screeching and crunching up on the hill and you giggling and bouncing in here."

Miggle made another creak and pretended to snore gently.

For a moment all was quiet except for the noise up on the ridge from the big digging machines they had christened the Elephants. Then: "I wish they would go away," Kit whispered. "It sounds awful. Worse than chalk scritching up the blackboard."

"Uh huh. Daddy says it's monstrous," Trish quoted impressively.

Alarmed, Kit wriggled closer to Trish. "There aren't *really* elephants up there? Or . . . or monsters? Are there?"

Trish giggled. "Of course not, silly. Daddy meant it's monstrous that those machines go all night long."

"Why do they, then?"

In a low, gloating voice Trish growled, "The better to gobble up . . . the mountain, you goop!" She and Kit giggled sleepily.

Chapter Two

Miggle could no longer hear the whispers in the loft. She yawned and curled up on her left side. High up the ridge the great digging machines seemed to trumpet and clank more dimly. But it wouldn't do to go to sleep. Not yet. Not while something bothered her, something off in a corner of her mind. Had she . . . no, the clues hadn't gotten mixed up. She had quadruple-checked. She punched her pillow into shape and yawned again. But the conviction that something was missing nibbled at the edge of her thoughts like a small mouse. No. Everything was perfect. Nothing left out. She could almost feel the wonderful walnut-shaped box in her hands, as big as . . . as an ostrich egg. It was as smooth as satin under the fingers, and with a warm sheen as dark as a hundred years. Mr. Dekany's eyes smiled while he soberly described the workings of the box.

"It is, you see, with the little brass hinges set inside, here, so that when it is closed, it looks to be a nutshell from out a dream. So large! No hinges to show, and the little lock, here (snap!), is hidden also. But you have only to push this small bump here (snick!), which is really a small wooden peg on a spring, you see, and so!"

"And did you *really* carve it all yesterday?" Miggle had marveled.

Mr. Dekany's eyebrows gathered together into a frown, but he had been pleased. "What else should I be doing yesterday, my dear young lady? Every day I do the same. Every day in the mill it was another sameness, and now they have retired me with a golden watch, why should I not carve all day? Ah, but you mean how?" The old eyes twinkled under the shaggy frown. "The shape in ten minutes I have peeled out of a block of pine that is not too soft. By after supper with the television, it is hollowed out and the look of the nutshell given it, so that I can sand and polish and rub while I watch the old films on the television. The old films I sometimes like, and the concerts, but the rest, fah! The rest, it is for those who have put their minds out to pasture. Hmph! But, I see, you do not ask about that but about the box. You think it would be large enough to hold a doll, eh?"

"No." Miggle had laughed. "I'm too old for dolls! And . . ."

" 'No, it is not large enough,' or, 'No, you are too old'?" The voice growled and the eyebrows fluttered up. "With the lathe I can make you ten dolls to put inside it, perhaps twelve, each doll inside another. Like little nests of boxes."

"Can you really? I've seen those. But none of them ever had more than six dolls, and they were awfully expensive. Could you *really* make twelve that fit like that?"

Mr. Dekany, for once, had smiled with his whole face.

"Yes, of course. But I tease you, which I should not. As for the box, last night I smooth it; this morning I fit the small hinges and the catch. Before lunch I stain and oil it. Just a bit ago I have been rubbing it in this soft old cloth. Now it is finished. But what to put in it, I do not know. My house is a box full of boxes." He waved an arm at the tidy sitting room with its sewing box and cigar humidor boxes and candy boxes and the "In" and "Out" and "To Be Forgotten" boxes on the desk. In the middle of the room there was a round table. If you lifted the top up as if it were a box lid, the table turned into a chair with a round halo of a back. Miggle knew, too, that not all of the books on the bookshelves were books. *The Tale of the Wandering Chicken Coop* was really a box, carved and painted to look like a leather-bound book. Mr. Dekany kept hollyhock seeds in that one. How many of the other books were boxes she was not sure.

"Heh? What do you say? If it were your box, what would you put into it?" Mr. Dekany's sharp eye seemed to rebuke her curiosity about the books.

"Well, I don't know." Miggle thought for a moment. "It would have to be something valuable, and I don't have anything valuable. Except my rock collection. There's a desert rose and a piece of real turquoise and an Apache tear in my rock collection. But I've got all my rocks stuck on a big piece of plywood. They're all labeled, and Daddy made a frame for it."

Mr. Dekany's eyebrows raised, and he said, "Ahh!" with a sigh of such great disappointment that Miggle suspected he might be teasing again. She could never tell.

"So you have nothing," he said. "Then I suppose I

must use it for rubber bands and bits of string. It is always good to have handy such things."

Miggle had suddenly remembered the key. She fished in the pocket of her blue jeans and brought up an object wrapped in paper toweling. "What about this? It's my treasure for this morning. I just found it. And since I don't know what it's for, it *might* be a treasure, mightn't it?"

"Hah! Let me see it." The old man unwound the paper toweling and held a brownish, crusty object in his hand. It looked rather like a broken key; a fairly large one. "You have been trying to clean it, eh? Where did you find it?"

"In the spring. That's why I like it, I guess. It's such a silly place to put anything. Do you suppose it's valuable? I thought it might be gold. See, where I scratched the stony stuff off, it *looks* gold."

Mr. Dekany shook his head. "Brass, perhaps, but I think not gold. No one makes a key of gold. It is too soft." He stood up and pushed his chair back. "But we will see. You come down into the basement where I have my tools, and we will see."

They had gone down into the tiny cellar. The shelf-lined walls were bright with whitewash and the jewel colors of glass jars of home-grown plums, cherries, beets, corn, and everything a garden and orchard can be asked to grow. On the workbench at the back, behind the furnace, Mr. Dekany chipped away the mineral deposit that coated the key. "Hah! It is very odd, this. You see here–it is like the crust which grows inside the teakettle. At least it is very old. I would not think it would gather so much of the minerals lying in your spring. It was inside? In the deep water behind the little door in the hill?"

"Yes." Miggle looked down at her fingernails, embarrassed. "We're not supposed to open the door and monkey around in there. Daddy says it stirs up the silt and makes our water gritty. But . . . I was curious. And I tried to be very careful. I used Daddy's minnow net and moved it around the bottom as slowly as I could. Then I found the key or whatever it is. And the water did look awfully muddy, so I stopped and shut the door and came away."

"Hmph. Your father must put a lock on the little door to keep the small two-legged animals out, as well as the four-legged ones. But look. It does not seem after all to be a key." He held it out in the palm of his hand. "A very good kind of brass, I think."

"Not gold?" Miggle was disappointed.

"No. It is very, very hard indeed. Even brass I had not thought should be so hard. And it has a softer color than India brass. Some polish rouge and the little buffing wheel, so, will make it gleam for you." He flipped a switch, and the small wheel hummed. Finally, he cleaned the last smudge of polish off on a bit of rag and handed the key—if it was a key—to Miggle. It looked like this:

The end was smooth. If it was a key, it was a very odd one, for clearly nothing had been broken off at the tip, and so it would have had to be a key without wards. The stem was not round or flat, either, but was grooved, so that from the tip end it looked like this:

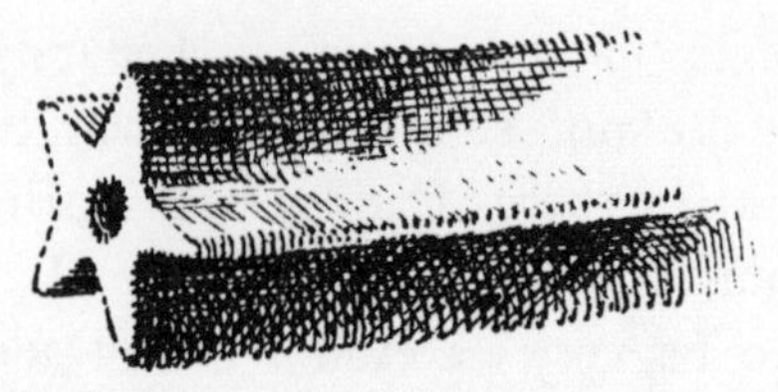

It was disappointing.

"It must be a piece off the decoration of something," said Miggle, very glum. They went up the stairs.

"From a brass bedstead, perhaps, you mean? Hah! It is possible, but I think not. Certainly, it is unusual. And I think, until you know, you might keep it safe in the walnut box, eh? Here. You are to take it." He thrust the beautiful box at her. "Hah! And now you go out to the kitchen garden and bother Mrs. Dekany, if you wish. I have much to do. I do not know why I should waste my valuable time with silly little girls. Hah!" He slammed the door behind Miggle before she could manage to finish saying thank you.

She had hidden the box so that Trish would not find it, and from time to time she had taken the key thing out and turned it over and over. It was no use. Some wind-up clocks, she knew, had keys with square shanks and no wards, but never, so far as she knew, star-shaped shanks. As she turned it over in the palm of her hand, the words turned over in her head: "Since I don't know what it's for, it *might* be a treasure, mightn't it?" But how to find out? Miggle had no idea where to begin. Arthur would have known. Miggle supposed she would end up asking him when he came, but she didn't like the thought of admitting she was stumped. And he might not even be interested. Or he might look at it casually and say it was . . . oh, a finial for on top of a lampshade.

Miggle peered at the little hole in the tip end. There weren't any screw threads, so it couldn't be a lamp finial. She tried the encyclopedia. It was very informative about keys, but none of the drawings looked at all like the whatsis. There were no clues in Mrs. Arthur's book of *1001 Decorative Motifs*. There wasn't a glimmer in the whole Arthur library. But she had found an old book, tucked behind a row of Trollope's novels, that put a gleam in her eye. It was bound in leather so old and crumbling that it left a reddish leathery dust on her hands and on her jeans where she had held it in her lap to look at the odd engravings. On the title page there was engraved a border of Greek columns and vases and fancy wrought-iron-looking curlicues. On one vase there was a picture of a man with a bull's head. Inside the border a prancing centaur held up a shield on which the title of the book was displayed: *Liber Monstrorum*. Something to do with monsters, Miggle guessed. Parts of the rest of the book were in the same strange language, but most of it was in quaint old-fashioned English. There were a lot of maps, too. It was just the kind of book old Dub would like. His sixth grade class had studied French, too. Maybe *Liber Monstrorum* was French.

Maps. Dub. Mysterious treasure. Clues. All at once the plan, the idea of a real treasure hunt, had fallen into place in Miggle's mind like the pieces of a picture puzzle that suddenly comes right. It had all fitted beautifully. That had been a week ago. But now that Arthur and Stevie and Kit were actually here, Miggle had this bothersome feeling that there was, so to speak, a puzzle piece missing somewhere. She yawned and turned to curl up on her right side. She was too sleepy to worry about it any more.

"Ssst! Memsahib! Memsahib Meegle! Ssst, please!"

Miggle opened one eye, warily.

"You come, Memsahib Meegle, please? You come 'long side M'longi, ssst?" The door was open, and a pale blur, which was Arthur Arthur in his pajamas on his hands and knees, beckoned in the darkness. "Ssst! You come 'long M'longi, see tribe of Tantor in Valley of the Moon." The blur backed out of sight.

Casting a cautious eye at the sleeping girls in the double bed, Miggle wriggled out of the deep feather mattress and slipped out through the hall and into the loft. A full moon flooded the floor and the boys' rumpled bed with light, but the high-pitched ceiling and its rough-hewn log beams were lost in shadow.

"Come look at your Elephants, Mig." Stevie made room for her on the wide window seat.

Dub pointed. "See, Missy! The new Valley of the Moon and all the greedy long-tooths with glassy, glary eyes."

Outside the window a narrow, seldom-used wooden stairway led from a tiny landing just above the sun-porch door down to the corner of the porch on the side near the barn. The back garden stretched away beneath them. Beyond the barberry hedge that marked the upper side of the chicken run, the orchard climbed up over a hill to meet the Wood where it flowed down from the ridge top and lapped around the edges of the farm. The moon silvered the treetops and turned the round pond below the spring into a bright mirror. But beyond the high treetops that marked the beginning of the Wood, there were strange new peaks, pale and shining, all in a jagged row below the moon.

"Golly!" Miggle's eyes widened, and she sat down with a plump.

"Shhh!" Arthur went back to close the door into the hall.

Stevie asked, "They haven't ever been this close before, have they?"

Miggle shook her head. "No," she said. "And they must have dug up all that strip since this morning. They must have struck a good rich patch in their old coal seam." She nodded thoughtfully, giving herself the air of one who knows much about the stripping process of mining coal.

Beyond the line of pale peaks, the great diesel-electric digging machines were close enough to be seen as they lifted their long necks and swung their heavy mouths up over the new ridge. Each wore a great spotlight at the topmost part of its boom, or neck. Metal screeched and cables squealed. The great mouths opened and dribbled dirt by the ton onto the jagged heaps.

Miggle pointed. "See that biggest one up there on the left—with the longest neck? It's big enough to hold two pickup trucks in that old bucket mouth."

Dub and Stevie stared at her, unbelieving.

"No, honest. Ask Daddy. One of the truck drivers told him. It has a whopping big cabin and engine on a turntable, and it moves around on big heavy treads—they call them cats. And this man said those little earth-biters up there eat twenty cubic yards at a mouthful and the big Elephant can take a hundred and twenty cubic yards at one time. I don't know how much that comes to in tons, but it sounds like an awful lot."

Dub figured swiftly in his head. A hundred and twenty

cubic yards. If a pickup truck was, say, fifteen to twenty feet long and. . . . He breathed out in a low whistle. "I suppose you *could* get two pickup trucks in it if you wanted to. No wonder they manage to dig fast enough to keep all those trucks scurrying all day long. Those big old Dodge trucks can carry over twenty tons, some of them, I think."

"They must have scooped out a really deep hole up there," said Stevie. "Except when they lift up to dump, about all you can see are those lights up on top. They must be sitting down in there pretty far."

"Uh huh," agreed Miggle. "What they do is, when they want to plow up a new stretch to uncover some more of the coal seam, they loosen the earth up with dynamite, and then the bigger Elephants move that loose dirt off somewhere else. When the coal is uncovered, the bulldozers and things load it into the trucks. They clean every smidgin of it up. You never see a bit of coal left around. We can go up tomorrow morning and I'll show you," she offered. "I know a good lookout point. You know, they've stripped a whole half mile or more along that seam since spring? From High Egg village over on the next ridge, looking back this way, it's like . . . like a wound in the Wood."

Miggle paused for effect, but the boys only nodded absent-mindedly.

"Anyway," she said, "it *is* a wound, sort of. Every day they make it worse with a big blast of dynamite and scraping away at it with their Elephants."

"Gosh, I sure wouldn't want to work for your old Mr. Minshew," Stevie said. "They must get bored. Sitting in that little cab thing and pulling levers all night long—just to eat an old hole in the side of a mountain."

Arthur leaned his forehead against the window. "They really are kind of like prehistoric monsters, chewing up trees by the roots and all. Monsters on White Oak Mountain!" he exclaimed in a deep voice. "Nassty ellafumps, like Rover says. Great hulking mastodons trodding down the trees."

"Mmm-hm. Monsters," echoed Miggle, sneaking a look at Dub from the corner of her eye and thinking of the book in the library below. "Crunching up the nice old Wood, nibbling along the fences, thinking how nice the orchard might taste. Or the barn. Or maybe Willy's doghouse, or Trumpkin."

"No-o-o-o-oh!" An ear-splitting wail came from the doorway. "Mama-a-ah!" Rover stood on the threshold in pajamas and bare feet, his blanket trailing after him along the floor. He had very good lungs for a two-year-old. He bellowed. The hall light flashed on, and Mrs. Arthur stumbled into the loft, having somehow wound up her feet in Rover's blanket.

"Dear, dear, dear!" she crooned, sitting down on the blanket and folding Rover in her arms. "What is it? What's the matter?"

All the answer she had was a jumble of wails and sniffles and monsters, gulps and doghouses and Trumpkin. Mr. Arthur appeared in the hall, moving dazedly toward the noise. He was followed by Trish and Kit. Groping, he switched on the loft's hanging lamp.

"All right. Who's been sticking pins in Rover . . . er, Morton, I mean?"

The younger girls giggled. Miggle, with a great effort, managed not to.

Arthur said, over the noise, "It's my fault, Uncle Owen. We were watching the strip mining and I got

Miggle to come in and, well, we were talking about the machines being like greedy monsters, coming closer all the time, and Mig said they'd like to be nibbling at the farm, and maybe Terwilliger's doghouse or Rover's puppy, and I guess old . . . Morton was listening at the door."

"Thank you, Dub . . . er, Arthur." Mr. Arthur bent down wearily. "All right, Morton. You can stop yowling. No one is going to eat Trumpkin. He's safe asleep in the barn. Your sister and the boys were just pretending. It's all right."

Rover subsided into shuddering snuffles, and Mr. Arthur picked him up so that Mrs. Arthur could untangle herself from the blanket.

"Owen, dear"–she sighed–"we'd better take him into bed with us or he'll never get to sleep. All the rest of you children, now, right back to bed with you." Mrs. Arthur folded the blanket, shooed the girls into the hall, and turned off the boys' light. "That strip mining has become the bane of my existence," she declared as she closed the door.

"What's a bane?" Stevie whispered.

"Dunno. Bane. It rolls on the tongue like the ding of doom," Dub intoned dramatically as he pulled a blanket up over their top sheet. The night was growing cool. "I'll look it up in the morning."

Rover dropped off to sleep almost immediately. Mr. Arthur whispered across him to Mrs. Arthur. "Vi? You awake? You know, it's funny the kids should get to talking that way tonight. I'd been half thinking the same thing myself. It's no make-believe. They *are* nibbling all around our edges. I was thinking–what if they go too deep?" He frowned. "Might cut off the water supply. Springs are funny things, you know. They can disappear overnight and pop up somewhere else. That heavy blasting could disturb the rock strata that carries the water, and we'd be high and dry."

Mrs. Arthur stared at the ceiling and listened to the distant squealing clatter.

In that moment just before sleep comes, Miggle realized what the missing piece was. If Dub *did* find the treasure in the walnut box and they *didn't* figure out what it was, or if it *did* turn out to be something disgustingly ordinary, she was in for it. The hunt would be worse than a wild-goose chase; it would be a big fat fake. Dub would be disgusted and superior and unbearable. A "silly busy-game Super-Deluxe-Colossal" he would call it and stomp off to go fishing, an amusement Miggle thought equally liable to be called a silly busy-game as there wasn't a fish in Mishannock Run nowadays large enough to keep. "Fishing" meant baiting hooks with johnny-craws, sitting like a stone for hours, catching dozens of finger-sized trout and throwing every one of them right back in. Silly. . . . Of course, she wouldn't *have* to tell that she had invented the treasure hunt. And the key-hickey was . . . it *had* to be real. "*Please* be real," she thought, thoroughly muddled. And while she was thinking it, she fell into a dream in which Mr. Dekany lived in a chicken coop that walked around on spindly legs. "Real *what?*" whispered Mr. Dekany as his house stepped through the door in the hill.

Terwilliger sat sleepless in front of his doghouse and howled at the moon and the noise on the hill.

Chapter Three

"Bane," said Arthur. " 'O.E. bana, bona; destroyer, destruction.' " He wrinkled his nose. "Wait a minute till I see what O.E. means." He turned to the list of abbreviations. " 'Old English.' Huh. Maybe it comes from the breaking of bones? Anyway, it's a darned good name for the stripping. If it isn't destruction to muck up the scenery and disturb the peace, I'll eat my . . ."

"Socks?" suggested Trish innocently as she gingerly made her way across the library-studio to the sun-porch door, carrying a large glass jar full of water.

" 'Hat,' I was about to say," corrected Dub with offended dignity. "Stephen, my boy, trip that wench."

Trish squealed and made the door with considerable speed and minimum spillage.

"So it's the Bane from now on," Miggle agreed.

"Let's take some sandwiches and a canteen of lemonade up there for lunch and have a formal naming or christening or whatever you call it," Stevie suggested. "We can throw rocks at it instead of using a champagne bottle."

"Can't," said Miggle. "Every noon while the Elephant

ıething like that? Do you suppose *wyrm* is the same
:m'?"

u mean they thought a dragon was a worm?" Stevie
eptical.

ıybe 'worm' didn't mean just earthwormy things
then," Miggle offered, sitting on the floor beside
r and hiding her crossed fingers behind her back.
t else is there?"

ıur turned the pages. "Aha! There's the old Mino-
And this one looks like Caliban. I like old Caliban.
was a great Caliban when they did *The Tempest*
." He looked up. "Why don't your folks ever get
elevision set fixed? We could get up early and watch
chaeology course and learn how to dig up Indian
ls and stuff like that."

gle shrugged. "You ask Mother. I gave up months
But we hardly ever watched it except in winter.
's too much to do." Casually, she turned the last few

hoa!" said Dub. "Go back one. There's something
ed on that back flyleaf. A piece of paper with some-
on it. There."

o, it's a map, isn't it?" said Stevie.

oks like it. Looks pretty old, too. Faded old brown
Dub observed. What they saw at the top of the paper
is:

men are off to lunch, they blast more coal loose with dynamite. But we're allowed up after lunchtime. Not in the Bane, but in the woods, I mean. Let's go then."

Dub slipped the dictionary back into place in the bookcase and took down a textbook-looking volume titled *Larger Mammals*. "Do you know," he said, opening it idly as he propped himself against the shelves, "that in the old beast books from the Middle Ages it says elephants haven't any joints in their legs, so they have to sleep standing up, leaning against trees? If you wanted to kill one, you just snuck up and chopped down the tree, and over they'd go."

"Oh, come on! They didn't really believe that, did they?" Stevie scoffed.

"Sure they did." Arthur flipped through the book and replaced it. "Dad says the people who wrote the books probably hadn't any more seen an elephant than the people who read 'em. And you ought to see some of the nutty pictures in the old manuscripts. They wrote all the books out by hand, you know, because it was before anybody had printing presses," he explained. "The elephants have silly little ears and trunks wide at the end like funnels. Dad has photographs of a whole slew of funny animal pictures out of old beast books for a book he's writing. It's about animal lore or something."

Miggle was uncomfortable. Dub always prowled along the bookshelves seeing what was new, but he hadn't even gone near the old leather-bound volume. "Well," she said, "our elephants never bother to go to sleep. And they lean on trees on purpose to push them over. Let's talk about something else. Or *do* something. The old Bane is a pain."

"The Bane's a pain!" echoed Stevie, hopping around

the desk with his hands clutched over his stomach. "A pain that will remain."

Arthur climbed up on the tall stool that doubled as a library ladder and beat time in the air with a ruler. "And the main crane will dig the vein in hope of gain!"

Kit and Trish left their paintings on the sun-porch worktable and came into the library to see what was going on. The advent of an audience inspired Stevie to an Indian shuffle around the stool. "But I complain, it isn't sane," he croaked.

"Oh, if that vein should deign to wane," caroled Dub, "uh . . ."

"Train? Strain?" Kit offered.

"Uh– It's plain they fain would trundle down the lane!" spouted Dub triumphantly.

"What about cane?" said Trish.

Not to be outdone, Miggle broke the stalemate by dropping to her knees and imploring, "Refrain! Restrain this vain drain upon your brain!"

Arthur teetered on the stool, and Stevie collapsed with laughter, clutching his stomach in earnest. "Abstain, I'm slain," he moaned.

"Hey, that's good," said Dub in admiration. "Old Stevie wins. I guess Miggle does, too. She got out five in one breath."

"Stevie's was best though." Miggle got up from the floor and flopped into an armchair, weak from laughter.

Trish and Kit went back to the sun porch and their paints. "They forgot 'rain,' too," said Kit, choosing a brush and adding a purple storm-cloud to her sky.

"Hi, what's this?" Dub clambered down from the stool, stepped across Stevie, and lifted down a book. "*Liber*

Monstrorum. I never saw this
did this come from?"

"Don't ask me," she said, harc
sound uninterested. She had dete
to give anything away either.

"It's got some great pictures. Lo

"A whosilisk?" Stevie asked.

Arthur ignored the interruptio
a griffin. Gory oysters! Look at t
carpet and spread the book open l
over on his knees and looked at the

"Ick! What is it?"

"Search me. *Amphisbaena,* it
description on the next page. At
It looks like the same stuff as Dad's

"You can't read it then?" Migg
the book did look interesting.

"Now if it was French . . ."
and looked so superior that th
really," he said, and pointed to t
livre. That's 'book.' Hey, yes! *L*
it's 'Book of Monsters' all right.
though." He flipped the pages.
dragon, see, and down here it sa
this beeft . . .' This *beeft?* What

Miggle bent to look. "Those ar
laughed. "They made s both wa
actly like *f*'s. You ought to kno
Declaration of Independence."

"Uh. I forgot. So it's, 'this bees
this wyrm was beleeved to seek ou
and to take it for hys own.' *Ycle*

or so
as 'wo
"Y
was s
"M
back
Arthu
"Wh
Art
taur.
There
on T
their
the a
moun
Mi
ago.
There
pages
"W
faster
thing
"H
"L
ink,"
was t

Beneath it was written in a spidery hand:

Should you aſk where it would be
Between the watters wide and narrow,
The firſt doth drowſe beneath the tree.
Should you wonder where it lingers,
Dig between the tall one's fingers,
Where the arrow . . .

The verse broke off where the bottom of the paper was discolored and torn. Miggle had thought that a very good touch if she did say so herself. The style of handwriting she had copied from that in an early entry on the flyleaf of the family Bible.

"Gee whiz," said Stevie. "It sounds like something out of a book!"

"It *is* in a book, dumbbell," said Miggle.

"Oh, you know what I mean, Mig. It sounds like something out of an adventure . . ."

"Where there are jewels," Dub prompted. "No, valuable documents! Buried on the estate and the rightful heir will be turned out in the cold if they aren't found in time. But—no kidding, it *could* be something important. Except this map might be of any place. It hasn't got any place names at all on it."

"Except 'A house.' Which is kind of silly. You can *see* it's a house," said Stevie.

It was impossible for Miggle to keep quiet. "But there's a period after 'A.' Maybe that means something."

"It means there's a period after 'A,' " said Stevie. "What do you mean, 'What does it mean?' "

Arthur turned back to look at the front flyleaf. "This book didn't come from Grandpa's library, that's for sure, or I'd have seen it before. Where is it from, Mig?"

"I really don't know," she answered honestly. "Mother's the one to ask. I think she just went down to the basement, but she won't mind if we come down now. She fired a batch of stuff last night so the kiln would be cool before the blasting at noontime."

Mrs. Arthur was an artist and had become well known as far away as Pittsburgh for her pottery—handsome stoneware vases and bowls and platters glazed in warm earth colors and blues. Several shops in the city and in Kennington carried her designs, but most of them were sold to the tourists who shopped at The White Rabbit, a tiny shop in the High Egg Village Inn. The coming of the strip mining had brought Mrs. Arthur more problems than noise and rattling windows. The first several weeks of blasting had broken dozens of pieces of greenware—bowls and pots that hadn't yet gone through the first firing that hardens them into what is called bisqueware. Twice the explosions had gone off while the kiln was full of bowls going through their second firing. They had rocked off their stilts and bumped together, and the glaze had stuck fast, so that when the kiln was cool, Mr. Arthur had had to come to the rescue with a chisel and mallet to loosen the solid clump of bowls from the floor of the kiln. Now there were doors on the drying shelves, and Mrs. Arthur's firings were carefully timed so that noon could explode without catastrophe in the cellar.

While the kiln finished its long cooling-off, Mrs. Arthur was mixing a new glaze for the next batch. When the children appeared on the stairs with their question about the old leather-bound book, she warned, "Don't come over here. There's clay dust all over the floor, and you'll track it upstairs."

men are off to lunch, they blast more coal loose with dynamite. But we're allowed up after lunchtime. Not in the Bane, but in the woods, I mean. Let's go then."

Dub slipped the dictionary back into place in the bookcase and took down a textbook-looking volume titled *Larger Mammals*. "Do you know," he said, opening it idly as he propped himself against the shelves, "that in the old beast books from the Middle Ages it says elephants haven't any joints in their legs, so they have to sleep standing up, leaning against trees? If you wanted to kill one, you just snuck up and chopped down the tree, and over they'd go."

"Oh, come on! They didn't really believe that, did they?" Stevie scoffed.

"Sure they did." Arthur flipped through the book and replaced it. "Dad says the people who wrote the books probably hadn't any more seen an elephant than the people who read 'em. And you ought to see some of the nutty pictures in the old manuscripts. They wrote all the books out by hand, you know, because it was before anybody had printing presses," he explained. "The elephants have silly little ears and trunks wide at the end like funnels. Dad has photographs of a whole slew of funny animal pictures out of old beast books for a book he's writing. It's about animal lore or something."

Miggle was uncomfortable. Dub always prowled along the bookshelves seeing what was new, but he hadn't even gone near the old leather-bound volume. "Well," she said, "our elephants never bother to go to sleep. And they lean on trees on purpose to push them over. Let's talk about something else. Or *do* something. The old Bane is a pain."

"The Bane's a pain!" echoed Stevie, hopping around

the desk with his hands clutched over his stomach. "A pain that will remain."

Arthur climbed up on the tall stool that doubled as a library ladder and beat time in the air with a ruler. "And the main crane will dig the vein in hope of gain!"

Kit and Trish left their paintings on the sun-porch worktable and came into the library to see what was going on. The advent of an audience inspired Stevie to an Indian shuffle around the stool. "But I complain, it isn't sane," he croaked.

"Oh, if that vein should deign to wane," caroled Dub, "uh . . ."

"Train? Strain?" Kit offered.

"Uh– It's plain they fain would trundle down the lane!" spouted Dub triumphantly.

"What about cane?" said Trish.

Not to be outdone, Miggle broke the stalemate by dropping to her knees and imploring, "Refrain! Restrain this vain drain upon your brain!"

Arthur teetered on the stool, and Stevie collapsed with laughter, clutching his stomach in earnest. "Abstain, I'm slain," he moaned.

"Hey, that's good," said Dub in admiration. "Old Stevie wins. I guess Miggle does, too. She got out five in one breath."

"Stevie's was best though." Miggle got up from the floor and flopped into an armchair, weak from laughter.

Trish and Kit went back to the sun porch and their paints. "They forgot 'rain,' too," said Kit, choosing a brush and adding a purple storm-cloud to her sky.

"Hi, what's this?" Dub clambered down from the stool, stepped across Stevie, and lifted down a book. "*Liber*

Monstrorum. I never saw this one before. Mig, where did this come from?"

"Don't ask me," she said, hardly looking and trying to sound uninterested. She had determined not to fib but not to give anything away either.

"It's got some great pictures. Look, here's a basilisk."

"A whosilisk?" Stevie asked.

Arthur ignored the interruption. "And a sea serpent and a griffin. Gory oysters! Look at this." He sat down on the carpet and spread the book open before him. Stevie walked over on his knees and looked at the indicated engraving.

"Ick! What is it?"

"Search me. *Amphisbaena*, it says. It's Latin. So's the description on the next page. At least, I think it's Latin. It looks like the same stuff as Dad's Latin books."

"You can't read it then?" Miggle was disappointed, for the book did look interesting.

"Now if it was French . . ." Dub raised his eyebrows and looked so superior that the others scoffed. "No, really," he said, and pointed to the title. "*Liber*, I bet, is *livre*. That's 'book.' Hey, yes! *Liber* like in 'library.' So it's 'Book of Monsters' all right. Some of it's in English, though." He flipped the pages. "Here: *Draco*. That's a dragon, see, and down here it says, 'In Englond of old this beeft . . .' This *beeſt?* What on earth is a *beeſt?*"

Miggle bent to look. "Those are old-fashioned s's." She laughed. "They made s both ways. See, they're not exactly like *f*'s. You ought to know. They're even in the Declaration of Independence."

"Uh. I forgot. So it's, 'this beest was yclept wyrm, and this wyrm was beleeved to seek out gold buried in the erth and to take it for hys own.' *Yclept* maybe means 'called' or something like that? Do you suppose *wyrm* is the same as 'worm'?"

"You mean they thought a dragon was a worm?" Stevie was skeptical.

"Maybe 'worm' didn't mean just earthwormy things back then," Miggle offered, sitting on the floor beside Arthur and hiding her crossed fingers behind her back. "What else is there?"

Arthur turned the pages. "Aha! There's the old Minotaur. And this one looks like Caliban. I like old Caliban. There was a great Caliban when they did *The Tempest* on TV." He looked up. "Why don't your folks ever get their television set fixed? We could get up early and watch the archaeology course and learn how to dig up Indian mounds and stuff like that."

Miggle shrugged. "You ask Mother. I gave up months ago. But we hardly ever watched it except in winter. There's too much to do." Casually, she turned the last few pages.

"Whoa!" said Dub. "Go back one. There's something fastened on that back flyleaf. A piece of paper with something on it. There."

"Hoo, it's a map, isn't it?" said Stevie.

"Looks like it. Looks pretty old, too. Faded old brown ink," Dub observed. What they saw at the top of the paper was this:

Beneath it was written in a spidery hand:

Should you aſk where it would be
Between the watters wide and narrow,
The firſt doth drowſe beneath the tree.
Should you wonder where it lingers,
Dig between the tall one's fingers,
Where the arrow . . .

The verse broke off where the bottom of the paper was discolored and torn. Miggle had thought that a very good touch if she did say so herself. The style of handwriting she had copied from that in an early entry on the flyleaf of the family Bible.

"Gee whiz," said Stevie. "It sounds like something out of a book!"

"It *is* in a book, dumbbell," said Miggle.

"Oh, you know what I mean, Mig. It sounds like something out of an adventure . . ."

"Where there are jewels," Dub prompted. "No, valuable documents! Buried on the estate and the rightful heir will be turned out in the cold if they aren't found in time. But—no kidding, it *could* be something important. Except this map might be of any place. It hasn't got any place names at all on it."

"Except 'A house.' Which is kind of silly. You can *see* it's a house," said Stevie.

It was impossible for Miggle to keep quiet. "But there's a period after 'A.' Maybe that means something."

"It means there's a period after 'A,' " said Stevie. "What do you mean, 'What does it mean?' "

Arthur turned back to look at the front flyleaf. "This book didn't come from Grandpa's library, that's for sure, or I'd have seen it before. Where is it from, Mig?"

"I really don't know," she answered honestly. "Mother's the one to ask. I think she just went down to the basement, but she won't mind if we come down now. She fired a batch of stuff last night so the kiln would be cool before the blasting at noontime."

Mrs. Arthur was an artist and had become well known as far away as Pittsburgh for her pottery—handsome stoneware vases and bowls and platters glazed in warm earth colors and blues. Several shops in the city and in Kennington carried her designs, but most of them were sold to the tourists who shopped at The White Rabbit, a tiny shop in the High Egg Village Inn. The coming of the strip mining had brought Mrs. Arthur more problems than noise and rattling windows. The first several weeks of blasting had broken dozens of pieces of greenware—bowls and pots that hadn't yet gone through the first firing that hardens them into what is called bisqueware. Twice the explosions had gone off while the kiln was full of bowls going through their second firing. They had rocked off their stilts and bumped together, and the glaze had stuck fast, so that when the kiln was cool, Mr. Arthur had had to come to the rescue with a chisel and mallet to loosen the solid clump of bowls from the floor of the kiln. Now there were doors on the drying shelves, and Mrs. Arthur's firings were carefully timed so that noon could explode without catastrophe in the cellar.

While the kiln finished its long cooling-off, Mrs. Arthur was mixing a new glaze for the next batch. When the children appeared on the stairs with their question about the old leather-bound book, she warned, "Don't come over here. There's clay dust all over the floor, and you'll track it upstairs."

She covered the mixing pot with a piece of plywood to keep dust out of the glaze and went to the corner sink to wash her hands. "No, the book hadn't been Grandpa Arthur's," she said, after taking a look at it, "nor Grandpa Griffith's." She had found it under a loose floorboard in the attic during spring cleaning and had put it at the back of the bookshelves, thinking that Uncle Tim might be interested in it. "He's the only one in the family who could read it." She smiled, returning the book to Dub.

"Whose book is it, then?" asked Dub. "Who left it in the attic?"

"Probably the Hinkses. Or perhaps the Amples before them. According to Mrs. Hinks, the Amples built the house and lived in it for over a hundred years. Still, the book does belong to us now, Arthur. When old Mrs. Hinks moved to California to live with her son, she signed the deed and said, 'There! You can have the lot!' With old Mr. Hinks dead, I don't think she could stand the house, poor thing. Too empty."

Knowing well how her mother could drift from one subject to another, Miggle headed her back toward the book. "What about the Amples? Weren't the first ones pioneers?"

Mrs. Arthur sat down on the bottom step. "You probably know as much about it as I do, dear," she answered. "I suppose you could call them pioneers, though the frontier had moved further west by then. As Mrs. Hinks told it, Nathan Ample cleared the land and sometime before 1820 built this house—or the main part of it, not the library and sun-porch end. We think they must have planted the big Douglas fir tree in the side garden. It's at least that old."

Arthur looked at the book thoughtfully. "But why would farmers have a book like this?"

"To read, dear." She smiled. "It is an unusual book, though. There might have been a schoolmaster in the family—someone who could read Latin. There's a Mr. Ample at Thrale High School even today, come to think of it. Why? Is it important?"

"Kind of. Somebody's fastened a map in the back of it, only it doesn't say where it's a map of."

"Let me see. I don't remember seeing any map. Mmm, yes, I see what you mean. It is vague, isn't it?" The spidery handwriting had a suspiciously familiar backward tilt to it. She remembered that Miggle had borrowed her sepia drawing ink and wondered what sort of game it was that had such an ambitious and complicated beginning. But she was rather pleased with the riddle-like quality of the verse and thought to herself how nice it would be if Miggle were only as perceptive about people as she was about words and "things." Mrs. Arthur decided to let the game take its course and turned back to her work with a parting suggestion. "Why couldn't 'A. house' mean Ample House?"

Arthur was at the top of the steps in a bound. "I bet it does! Thanks, Aunt Vi," he called back down the stairwell. "Come on, you guys."

"Lunch will be ready in half an hour," Mrs. Arthur called after them.

Miggle and Stevie followed close behind Arthur, up into the hall and back to the library. There Arthur eased the map loose from the flyleaf at the back of the old book and spread it out flat on the desk. "It sure isn't much of a map. If it *isn't* this house, we'll never find out where it is.

There must be a million houses by roads with creeks somewhere near."

Stevie pointed. "But if it is this house, that one on the left could be the Trickle and the other one would be Mishannock Run."

"Right." Dub chewed at his lip. "But even that doesn't help much. They're 'watters wide and narrow' all right. But *what* tree? There must be loads of tall ones around. See, maybe those spots on the map are trees, but if this was written all that long ago, for all we know the right tree might have been cut down."

They trooped outside by way of the sun porch. Trish and Kit followed from curiosity, and when they had seen the map and heard the riddle, Trish asked, very sensibly, what it was a map *for*. No one knew, of course, and under such a practical challenge, the boys' interest began to lag a bit. Miggle began to be uneasy, for, after all, the *not* knowing was to be the point of the whole thing—the finding out what the treasure was. Since she was sure neither what the key thing was nor whether it was valuable, she had been particularly careful to be absolutely fair and honest in the clues by calling it 'it.' Now she wished she'd made the first clue more tempting. The box was beautiful and a treasure even if the brass thing was a . . . a lamp finial. She shouldn't have put the other tree dots on the map. How, she wondered, could she let them know that the ancient fir in the side lawn was the right tree?

Dub was saying, "O.K., say the map's really old, though it could have been stuck in there anytime before. . . . When did the whosises—the Amples—move away from here?"

Miggle roused herself. "I'm not sure. But old Mrs. Hinks told about moving here after the Johnstown Flood, and that was a long time ago," she said.

"It was in 1936 or 1937. Unless she meant the one in 1889," offered Stevie. The Griffiths lived in Johnstown.

"I don't think she was that old," said Miggle.

"Anyway, it must be older than 1936," said Dub. "I'm sure people must have stopped making f's for s's a good long while before then. Right. Which means we're in a pickle. A hundred years ago the trees that are big now must have been pretty little, and the ones that were big then must now be gone for lumber and things. Dad says in the old days the whole East was forest, and a squirrel could travel a thousand miles without touching ground. If he wanted to, that is. But all that got cut down, and everything in the woods has grown up since."

Miggle saw that she had either made the clue too vague or the game more complicated than she had realized. It wouldn't do. The girls were looking bored. "What about the arrow?" she said. "There's something about tree roots and an arrow."

"What about it?"

"You mean we've got to go around looking at old tree roots?" Stevie frowned."

"No," said Miggle, bravely taking the plunge. "But lots of trees around here don't have roots that look like fingers. Except our old pine tree. It's got lots. And it's a kind that doesn't grow around here naturally. Daddy thinks the Amples must have planted it. And look . . ." She pointed to the tree and then to the map, which Dub held. "That mark right there must be it."

"Well," admitted Dub, "it *is* almost exactly midway between the Trickle and the Run. Maybe that's what the poem means by 'between.' "

"Yes, yes!" Miggle was delighted. "Let's look."

"What'll we dig with?" asked Stevie.

"Rover's spoons!" said Trish. "Mother gave him some big old spoons to use in the sandbox. I'll go get them." She ran to the sandbox at the side of the sun porch and was returning with three large battered serving spoons when Rover saw her. He pushed Trumpkin, the basset pup, back into the dog run and ran after her.

"Mine! My spoons!" he protested. "Give 'em to me. They're mine."

Miggle was about to scold him for being greedy, but Kit caught at his hand just as he was about to fling himself on Trish. "You can help, too, Rover," Kit soothed. "No, don't hit Trish. Trisha, give him one. Let Stevie and Dub have the other ones, and we can help Rover if he'll let us." She gave the offended Morton a hug, which he grudgingly acknowledged by accepting a spoon and following the others across the driveway and into the side yard. Trish handed the spoons to the boys reluctantly.

"Are we going t' dig up the tree?" Rover asked.

The tree was broad and thick and tall enough to be safe from serving spoons. It took Arthur and Stevie together, with arms outstretched, to measure around its girth. It must have been at least eighty feet tall, and its branches swept out thickly, the lowest ones sweeping the grass almost twenty feet away from the trunk. The shade underneath the branches made it seem like a large, cool room full of green light that was sunshine filtered through millions of fir needles. The ground was soft and springy, carpeted by all the layers of needles that had fallen since the tree was a sapling. No grass would grow there, what with the shade and the smothering needles. Gnarled and twisted roots humped out in all directions from the center.

"They're *all* pointing somewheres," said Trish. "What's the bit about the arrow again?"

"It fell to earth, I know not where?" Stevie offered.

"Oh hush! What is it, Dub?"

"Um . . . 'between the tall one's fingers, where the arrow . . .' et cetera, et cetera. It doesn't sound as if it's the fingers doing the pointing but something else. Everybody look around and see if there's any shape or stone or anything that looks like an arrow."

"Those old spoons aren't going to be enough if we really have to dig," said Miggle. "I'll go out to the chicken coop and get the shovel." Better, she thought, to be innocently out of the way and let one of the others find the arrow.

"Not a shovel." Dub frowned. "We don't want to slice up any roots. See if there's anything smaller."

"Yup! There's a trowel and a little spade, I think," agreed Miggle. She sped off under the branches and into the sunshine. Arthur was faintly surprised. Miggle usually argued before she did anything that hadn't been her own idea. He would have expected her to be leaping from one root to another, wanting to be first to find whatever was to be found. Heck, maybe she was reforming. Arthur shrugged and scanned the ground. Even unreformed, he supposed she was better than most girls. She was interested in the right things even if she was silly. He thought of Linda Vincent, a girl in his class. She smudged her eyes all up and ironed her hair and said, "Oh, *reely?*" all the time with her eyebrows up. Dumb.

"That? That's not an arrow," Kit was saying.

"You want to bet?" said Stevie. "Dub, look here! See, where these two roots come together. The space in between is shaped just like an Indian arrowhead. What d'you think?"

It did, in fact, look like a roughly shaped arrowhead of the type once common to the area. Arthur whooped, and he and Stevie joined Rover, who had begun digging as soon as Stevie had pointed out the spot. Pine needles flew, and the thick rich humus beneath came up in clumps. If there had been any indications of Miggle's tampering, the evidence would have been scattered by Rover's first efforts or overlooked in the enthusiastic scrabble of spoons that followed. About eight or so inches down, they struck earth and began to proceed more carefully. With their hands the girls scooped out the loose black humus of ancient pine needles, making one pile and beginning another for the soft clayey earth that followed.

"Dub? What should we be looking for?" asked Trish dubiously.

"Anything. I don't know. Anything people usually bury, I suppose. Money, or papers. I guess it wouldn't be jewels. Unless the Amples were jewel robbers on the side."

Kit was carefully crumbling the dirt that Trish scooped from under the flying spoons. Her fingers closed upon something flat and hard. "Could it be something little and flat?" she asked.

"Why, what is it?"

She rubbed the dirt off and scratched at it with a fingernail. "I don't know. It's all waxy and funny."

She handed it to Arthur, who turned it over and peered at it. "It is wax, I think." He pulled out his pocketknife and opened the blunt-ended bottle-opener blade. The waxy coating scraped off easily, and with a soft ripping sound the rotten silk underneath gave and peeled away with it.

Miggle returned to find Rover still digging and the four others, heads together, bent over Kit's find. She dropped the trowel and spade with a clatter that startled them all.

"We found another clue!" said Trish, her blue eyes dancing. "Kit found it."

"It's more poetry," Stevie said.

"And screwy. There's something peculiar going on here," Dub said, puzzled. "Whatever it is we're looking for must be horribly valuable or important for anyone to have gone to such trouble and mystification. And it must have been meant to be found. If whoever hid it meant to hide it for good or to dig it up again himself, he wouldn't have bothered with clues. Here, take a look." He handed Miggle a dirty, battered piece of metal on which, when it was tilted to catch the light, there could be seen the words:

Sit you mid the watters
And aſk the mountains daughters.

"What do you think it means?" she said, handing it back.

"All I can think of is Mishannock Run," he said. "It's got to be that. The Trickle's too little for anyone to sit in the middle of it without damming it up."

"Besides," said Stevie, practically, "the arrow points that way."

Trish was hopping up and down on one foot. "I know! I know what it is! I bet that old arrow is pointing right at it. It's that rock . . . Throne Rock. It is!"

Miggle was surprised. She had not noticed before, but the arrow shape did seem to be in a direct line with the part of the Wood where Mishannock Run churned around Throne Rock and dropped over the little falls. She wondered how she could have missed it. "If it was a snake, it would've bit me," she muttered.

"What?"

"Mm, nothing." She hadn't realized she had spoken aloud. "Rover, stop digging," she snapped to hide her confusion. "We've found what we were looking for."

Arthur groaned. "But we can't go *look*. We'd have to cross the Bane if we went off in that direction, and it's almost noon." He was as interested and eager as the others but sat very still and straight, his dark eyes shining. Like a knight off to seek the Holy Grail, Miggle thought with a guilty twinge. She would have felt better if he were more . . . well, more like Stevie, itching to be off on a lark. After all, it was only a game. Even a *real* treasure hunt was only a game. She crossed her fingers. The box. That was treasure. So this was a real game. But then the words "real" and "game" went around and around and made a muddle in her head, and she couldn't make out what she was worrying about.

Stevie did a headstand. "But we can go up after lunch. We'll have a race."

"No fair!" Trish and Kit objected in unison. "We can't run as fast as you can," said Trish. "And besides, I guessed it. I say we all go together."

"Me, too," said Rover.

"No," Miggle answered firmly. "You have to take your nap after lunch, same as always." She began to dust off his overalls.

As the others got up and brushed themselves off, they heard Mrs. Arthur ringing the old brass schoolbell for lunch. And then the ground shook beneath their feet. A flowerpot crashed down the front-porch steps and rolled into the driveway. The house shuddered lightly on its foundation, and the bell gave one more faint clang. It sounded as if hailstones were pattering through the thick branches of the old tree.

"Crumbs!" Dub exclaimed.

The roar of the blast echoed across the fields to High Egg Ridge and back. Stevie made his eyes wiggle as if they were vibrating from the shock. The girls took their fingers out of their ears and dazedly followed Rover toward the back door. Mrs. Arthur was sitting on the back steps, holding the bell in one hand and the handle of a shattered glass pitcher in the other. She gestured glumly toward a wide puddle on the sun-porch floor.

"Have some lovely lemonade," she said.

Chapter Four

Rover had his milk and sandwiches in the kitchen while Miggle and the boys mopped up the sun porch. Trish and Kit squeezed more lemons, for somehow there wasn't a drop of milk left after Rover had his. "And the milkman brought three half gallons this morning. One of you must be a milk fiend," marveled Mrs. Arthur.

She sat at the telephone desk in the corner by the refrigerator and dialed Mr. Arthur's office at the Kennington Steel Mills. Soon she was giving him a vivid account of the lemonade disaster. There had been other casualties as well—a basin of clay "slip" left too near the edge of a worktable had made a sloppy and dangerously slippery mess of the basement floor. Earth and stones from the Bane had showered on the roof. Several shingles were knocked loose, and the lawn was littered with bits of rock. The children fortunately had been sheltered by the old fir tree. No, everything was fine now, she assured him. Rover had been with the other children and not, as usual, in the dog pen. He was now on his second sandwich. Yes, it could very well have been serious. She was quite angry, both about the glass pitcher—it had been Grandmother Arthur's—and about the clay slime all over the cellar. "Yes," Miggle heard her say, "*do* call Rob Padgett. He'll know exactly what we should do. It does no good at all to talk to either of these men here or to Mr. Minshew's main office. I know that man just sits there in his fat leather chair up in Pittsburgh and smiles and nods at the telephone as if I weren't on the line at all. 'Silly exaggerating female,' I suppose he thinks."

"Mr. Padgett's a lawyer," Miggle whispered. "Sally Padgett's in my class," she added, as if that added to Mr. Padgett's impressiveness.

Fresh lemonade, made with an alarming amount of sugar, was on the sun-porch table when Mrs. Arthur had finished at the telephone. Returning to the kitchen, she sent Miggle and the salad out with a request that lunch begin without her. Then she wiped away Rover's mustache of milk and whisked him upstairs for his nap. Fifteen minutes later she returned to brew herself a cup of tea and rejoin the children. The lull after the explosion had passed, and their excitement ran high. Mrs. Arthur was a willing listener to the jumble of details that poured out on all sides about clues and treasures and riddling poems. At the mention of the arrow, she noticed with interest Miggle's faint frown of puzzlement.

She smiled. "It seems very eager to be found, doesn't it? Don't swallow without chewing, Stevie dear. There's no rush. And please, I'd rather none of you went up into the Wood until after one o'clock, just in case. They might not think the last blast was big enough," she said, crossing her eyes comically, but so quickly that only

Stevie saw. He hiccuped violently while she continued as calmly as if she had done nothing. "They might give us another for good measure. And I'm going to ask that you stay out of the—what is it you were calling it? The Bane? It certainly is that! But do stay well out of it today. Tomorrow is Saturday, and it will be quite deserted. You can explore it tomorrow if you must."

"Oh, that's all right," Miggle agreed. To the cousins she explained, "We can get to Throne Rock without going up the trucking road past the end of the Bane. There's a path in the Wood, or we can go along the Run itself."

"What's that you've put in the lemonade, dear? Mint?"

Trish nodded. "Um hm. There was a bunch of fresh mint in a jar of water in the refrigerator. It wasn't for something special, was it?"

"No. But how nice. . . . Did one of you pick it?" As none of them had, she raised her eyebrows and drank up her tea. "Do you suppose I did? I know I'm absent-minded, but I hadn't thought it was that bad. Horrors!" She returned to the kitchen with a tray of empty plates and came back with the dessert.

For dessert there were crisp walnut cookies and dishes of lemon sherbet. Trish and Kit wrapped their cookies neatly in paper napkins for eating in the woods. The boys, knowing it was a good time to disappear, dashed upstairs to find and fill canteens for the expedition. The girls cleared the table. Miggle, drying dishes under protest while her mother washed, almost dropped the second pitcher in her rush to be finished by one o'clock. As the treasure hunters gathered at the sun-porch door, Mrs. Arthur suggested that they take Terwilliger along since he would be bound to howl for half an hour if he saw them go off without him. Willy was good company, so they willingly detoured by way of the dog pen. Rover's basset puppy, Trumpkin, stayed behind. He was too young and his legs were too short.

With a fleeting envy Mrs. Arthur noticed how very quickly the house and garden emptied of adventure, grew quiet and ordinary. With her eyes narrowed thoughtfully, she smiled to see the old library rug lose its glow of Ispahan. The walls simmered down from a peacock shimmer to a sedate washed-out blue. The bookshelves shrank from a strange and unexplored realm to a familiar and dusty collection of travel books and novels. Instead now, she thought, the orchard would be a kingdom of apple towns and the middle meadow a prairie dotted with Pawnee lodges. Or the Wood might no longer be a green cloak over White Oak Ridge but, instead, a forest in Logres. Then she shrugged and turned back to the basement and work—the feel of the clay and the shimmer of colors that danced from her imagination onto deep bowls and into fragile goblets for wine or bright water.

The trail through the Wood was even more quiet than the house. It parted from the road fifty or sixty yards beyond the lower pasture, not far from the point at which the crab-apple thickets blended into the Wood itself. As soon as Miggle had pointed out their path, Terwilliger was off into the Wood, racing ahead to sniff at intriguing trails and to push his nose into promising holes and thickets. The children hurried behind, quiet under the spell of coolness and rustling stillness. Turning to look at each other, they shared silent laughter at the sight of Willy's floppy, still puppyish gait and his joy in finding them still following when he came bounding back. He was the sort of dog some people impolitely call Heinz, but was for the most part a mixture of Dalmatian and Weimaraner. No one could remember ever having seen a dog quite like him. His coat was the silver-beige color of the Weimaraner, but it was dappled like a fawn's, with a few odd patches of white and spots of black for variety. He kept the puppyish manners, the grin, and the quizzical cock of the head of the Weimaraner, but had the smaller feet and the slim elegance of his Dalmatian mother. His eyes were silver.

"Ho! Look, he's sent up a quail." Dub pointed. It was the first bird they had seen since leaving the road. There were, oddly, few squirrels to be seen and no chipmunks. The farther into the Wood the path led them, the less they heard the calling of crows high above the treetops or the soft rustle of small animals under the leaves and in the laurel thickets. After a while they met and crossed the dirt road that farther uphill branched left to the Bane and right to the township reservoir. There were no trucks on the road, but the sound of the Elephants had started up again beyond the high ground off to their left.

Ahead they heard the ringing of the stream among its stones. Very shortly, the trail wound below a willow thicket, bringing them to a mossy shelf beside the Run. The path had been made by deer and stepped off the bank into the shallows to begin again upstream on the opposite side. The children, however, chose to go farther up, to a deeper spot where they could cross by way of the flat-topped stones that bulked up out of the swift and shadowed water.

Trish brought up the rear. Once across, she called, "Not far till the reservoir, Miggle. You better catch Willy and hold him so he doesn't decide to go swimming."

"I know. I was *just* going to, as a matter of fact."

"You were not. I bet you weren't."

"I was, *too*, Trish Arthur. You keep quiet. Besides, *you* pushed him in last time." Miggle was feeling an uneasiness that she could not put a name to and tried to cover it with a lofty assurance. "It's *my* dog and *my* path. I discovered it."

"That's what you say."

"Oh, shut up!" Miggle wiped her forehead with the back of her hand. It left a damp gray smudge. The air was close and warm.

Unruffled, Trish unwrapped a cookie and said to Kit, "Daddy says even if we aren't on the township water line, we ought to remember that nobody who is wants to drink Willy's bathwater." They laughed and shared a broken cookie. Soon the noise of the machinery thickened and vibrated among the trees, so that the children were forced to raise their voices to be heard. The air seemed heavy and unmoving despite the rushing water of the stream. Usually, it was cool and fresh by the water even on the hottest day.

Miggle stumbled. All five of the children walked more slowly. Arthur and Stevie, as before, were keeping a sharp eye out for quail and deer; but the urgency all had felt over the riddle about Throne Rock had evaporated into the dull air.

"It's the noise," Dub said loudly. "It's wrong. The Wood doesn't like it at all."

They walked on slowly, the Run still on the left, until an object floating in one of its quiet pools caught Dub's eye. "Hello! Look at that." Stevie followed him to the edge of the water. Miggle turned, frowning, but did not move after them.

"It's only an old dead fish. Leave it alone and come on. I want to find the . . . I want to get to Throne Rock even if you don't." She said it without really feeling it.

"Aren't you the pill!" Stevie looked up from the fish. He had been feeling an odd sleepiness, a dreaminess, as they came deeper into the Wood, but now he shook it off.

"You know what this is, don't you?" Dub asked, frowning.

"It's a dead fish," Miggle snapped. "What do *you* think it is? Oh, come on and quit fooling."

"Of course it's a dead fish. I didn't mean it was a pineapple. But it oughtn't to be dead. That's the point. There's not a mark on it. And look at the water. I know it used to be clear as crystal because I remember sitting on the bank down by the bridge and watching grains of sand shift deep on the bottom. But there's a kind of yellowish cloud in it all along here, as if somebody had been mucking it up. Or worse."

Stevie nodded in violent agreement. "Sure. I bet a hundred dollars the old fish got polluted."

"Poisoned," Miggle corrected. "Fish get poisoned. Water gets polluted. Anyhow, what's it got to do with the price of eggs in China? Besides, it smells. Throw it away."

Arthur saw that Trish and Kit held back from the bloated trout along with Miggle. Girls! he thought in disgust. But he threw the fish in a high arc and saw it disappear beyond a clump of laurel. It hadn't exactly smelled like a rose, and the odor lingered on his hands. He wiped them on his jeans.

"Don't you see?" he urged. "The noise and vibration and the heavy traffic up the old road have scared all the birds and animals away, and I bet the Bane has something to do with the water going bad. This whole part of the

Wood feels half dead. Kind of smothered." He shivered in the warm, musty air.

Miggle looked around. Her attention had at first been centered on making a beeline for Throne Rock. Then, mixed with it, there had been a contrary urge, a growing reluctance, a sense that something unpleasant, even fearful, lay ahead to be faced. Miggle did not like being confused and usually avoided it by being doubly positive. Now she abandoned her bossiness in surprise at the deadness of the Wood. It *was* the Wood that was wrong. Its musty closeness had drifted through her thoughts without her noticing, but once she took notice, she was free of it. The Wood was as still as if no breeze had ruffled it in months. Dust lay faintly on all the leaves.

She laughed. "It's just like old Mrs. Skipple's front parlor, except for the dust sheets." Miggle had gone to young Miss Skipple for piano lessons. "I used to peek in while I was waiting in the hall. It had a queerish, dead, flat smell and sheets on all the furniture and heavy old velvet drapes and dried flowers. It wasn't even used on Sundays." She turned, leading the way back onto the path and uphill. "After her mother died, Miss Skipple had the house all done over and the front parlor all green and white like Wedgwood. But she had to keep the windows open or that musty old smell came back. Hey!" She turned to ask Arthur, "You don't suppose the Wood will be like this always, do you?"

"If there's any of it left, you mean. I dunno. It's kind of hard to redecorate a wood. They could fill in the Bane and smooth it over and plant trees. Isn't there a law that says they have to?"

Miggle pulled a long face. "Daddy says lots of times

they figure it's cheaper to pay the fine than to smooth it back like before and plant trees. They have to fill in all the holes, I think, so they don't fill up with water." She shivered. "Before they had to do that, people could fall in and drown. In the old stripping, down toward the highway, there was an awful hole, and a fellow and his girl fell in and drowned. They went on a moonlight walk without enough moonlight, and the dirt's so ashy and crumbly that if you start downhill, you just keep on going like an avalanche."

Arthur thrust his fists in his pockets. "Somebody ought to stop the whole thing—and put everything right."

"It's pretty hard to un-pollute fish," put in Stevie.

"Water," corrected Miggle absent-mindedly. The boys grinned and made faces at her back.

The path brought them to the shallow edges of the Run, and they crossed again, stepping from rock to rock. Trish ran ahead, and in a very few minutes led them into the open and up a short weed-covered slope onto the breast of the township dam. Some hundred yards above the Bane, it sparkled in a clearer air than the Wood below. It was small, shaped like a large drop of water, and overhung by birch and pines on all but the northeast side where the children stood. There a narrow rutted road followed the crest of the dam, crossing the Run by a log bridge where it came down the dam spillway. The road beyond curved up under the trees and faded back into the Wood near the spot where the upper stretch of Mishannock Run emptied into the dam on the west. The road went on but had seen so little use in recent years that spring rains had in the steeper places scrubbed away gravel and earth, leaving the sharp edges and mossy backs of great boulders.

Tufts of fine grass grew wherever there was a crack to be found. From above, branches reached down to weave a roof across the way. On the less steep stretches the grass made a deep feathery carpet.

From the clearing the old road looked like a cool tunnel filled with green light. Arthur had explored it during earlier summers at the farm, following its ancient branching tracks until each one circled back to join some newer road or ran to earth in some high ridge clearing. But now, for some reason, it had a different air, a greener light. He slid a glance at Miggle, who stood beside him, one hand on Willy's collar, the other wound around with the slack of his leather leash. She noticed something, too, but was distracted by Willy's lunges toward the upper road. Stevie, apparently looking for fish, was stretched flat on the log bridge with his head and shoulders out over the water. Trish and Kit were trying, girl-fashion, to skip stones across the dammed-up water, though they sank at the first splash every time.

Miggle wrinkled her brow and nose in puzzlement. She had the sensation that she was for the first time actually seeing this part of the Wood as it was, as the whole Wood once had been. She caught Arthur's glance.

"Funny," she said. "It seems, well . . . *greener* than it was the other day. But I guess that it's just that after the dusty old Wood below, we just . . ."

"Maybe we just feel its woods-ness more?" Dub nodded. "I guess so. Go ahead, you lead on. The others'll come fast enough when they see us go. I think we're all nuts, you know. We come out jabbering about a treasure hunt, and it takes us half an hour to go half a mile. Some hunt!"

"No, you go first." Miggle hung back. "I think there's somebody in there. Look! See there–way up, just where the road bends. I saw him move."

Arthur ran across the log bridge, across the rattling stones on the upper shore, and a short way into the Wood.

"Hey! Hey, you!" he called, his voice echoing thinly. "You, wait a minute."

Terwilliger strained at his leash, pulling Miggle along. The others, curious, came after, drying their hands on their clothes.

"It was a boy," Dub announced. "He ran away. Who do you suppose it was?"

"Don't ask me." Miggle shook her head. "Nobody lives up around here. There are some cottages farther north, on an old road up from Goggle. People come there summertimes, but we don't know any of them."

"Maybe it was Sticky Barnes," Trish offered. "He gets on the school bus a ways beyond the Run. I don't know where he lives. He's mean. If he's up in those old woods, don't you tell him what we're doing. He'll spoil everything."

"Sticky's only eight," Miggle interrupted. "Whoever it was is bigger than that. Wasn't he?" She bent to unfasten the leash from Willy's chain collar but kept fast hold of the collar itself.

Dub nodded. "He was as big as me. I *think*. I mean, he moved so fast I didn't get a good look."

Chapter Five

Up from the dam, the road ran parallel to the Run for about fifty yards, and the children moved along it quickly but cautiously. They saw no one. As the road bent away from the sound of the stream, they moved left through the trees and down through the ferns to the Run. A fall of rocks had made a natural dam, a round shallow pool that overflowed in a dozen tiny falls to become deep and swift again on the way downhill. A fisherman in waders could easily step out to sit facing the pool on high-backed Throne Rock in the middle of the dam, but for anyone in bare legs and tennis shoes it was more difficult. The water was bitterly cold. Excitement had returned with the smell of laurel and pine in the sweet green light. The sound of the Elephants was dimmed, shut out by a fold of hill between the Bane and the upper Run.

Arthur slipped off his sneakers and socks and, using an overhanging branch to steady himself, stepped out onto the rocks that dammed up the Run. Foaming water spilled between his feet.

"Yoicks, it's cold," he gasped. In a moment he was seated on the rock in the middle, ruefully rubbing his feet. "What was that rhyme again?" he called.

Miggle opened her mouth and shut it quickly. She let go of Terwilliger's collar and busied herself with winding up the leash and sticking it away in a hip pocket.

Trish dug into the pocket of her shorts and came up with the small metal plaque. "Sit you mid the waters and ask the mountain's daughters," she read out.

"What's the mountain's daughters?" asked Kit. "Stones? They're bits off the mountain, anyway."

"Naw," Stevie drawled. "It couldn't be rocks. Daughters are too mushy."

"You just wish you'd thought of it first," said his sister. She stuck her tongue out and prudently retreated behind a tree.

Dub whistled. "Cut out the clowning and help, you two. O.K., let's say it does mean the rocks. How do I ask them? And what? And which rocks? I see stones all over the bottom of the pool and rocks all the way upstream."

He squinted at the pool and then up at the leafy roof. "Wait a minute. No. . . . There's something–a stone–out from the middle there that glimmers like there's sunshine hitting it. Only it can't be. Sunshine, I mean." He stood up, peered, and again sat down.

"Steve, old thing. Take off your shoes and hop out into the liquid."

"Why me? You've already got yours off."

"Because. Because I can't see it when I'm not sitting down. Can you see it over there?"

"Nope." Stevie looked at the water dubiously. "Aah, O.K."

He sat down on the bank to take off his shoes and socks. Trish and Kit moved upstream, crossed at a narrow point, and came back along the other side of the pond. From their exchanges it was clear that the glimmering rock was not visible except from Arthur's vantage point.

Miggle fought the urge to blurt, "No, no! It's under the seat. It's not in the pond. It's under the Throne!" She was sorry she had ever thought of maps and clues. First there was that funny thing about the arrow, then the smothering Wood slowing them up, and now this clear green woodsness that seemed to sharpen ears and eyes to an unaccustomed fineness. Willy moved close and nuzzled her hand. Miggle sat down slowly on a rock beside him and put her arm around his neck. She knew, without knowing how she knew, that the clue *was* in the middle of the pond, that it no longer lay under the Throne. It was very confusing. She thought back to the words scratched so painstakingly upon the copper. If you were sitting on the Throne, you wouldn't really think of that as sitting on the mountain's daughters. You wouldn't look under it if you were sitting on it. What had put the words into her head? Mountain's daughters. It sounded more like elves or nymphs or something than rocks.

Stevie was up to his knees in mid-pond, moving left or right or backwards as Arthur directed. When he reached the spot Arthur indicated, he lifted up a round flat stone the size of a plate and underneath, in what seemed almost a shallow rock bowl, he found the second small flat packet. "I don't understand," Miggle whispered. Willy turned his head and generously kissed her neck and ear. "Do *you* understand?" she asked; but Willy only grinned his grin and turned to watch the others with his silver eyes.

"Dub, your old rock's just an old rock," Stevie said. "It doesn't shine a bit." He dropped it with a huge *splat* and splashed noisily back to the bank, followed by Arthur, who chose to come through the water this time as the quickest way. The younger girls crowded close to watch Stevie peel open and scrape clean the bit of metal. Miggle stayed by Willy, half fearing that the words of the clue might be different somehow, or wrong; that the game might no longer be hers.

"What does it say? What does it say?" Kit and Trish jumped up and down.

"Hey, keep off my stuff!" Stevie handed the little plaque to Arthur and bent to retrieve his shoes and socks.

The plaque read:

I delved deep to warm keep

Arthur passed it to the younger girls, who puzzled over it and then handed it on to Miggle. With warm relief that was mingled with an unaccountable twinge of disappointment she saw that it was just as she had made it, even to the long scratch where the tool had slipped on the last p.

"I bet I know what it is," she said, thinking to take firm hold of the game. If it was to be hurried, *she* would hurry it. "There's only one thing you can dig up around here that can warm you up when it's cold . . . coal! What else *could* it be?"

Dub and Stevie looked at each other dubiously. "Well, we see what you mean," Dub answered. "But that's not exactly what the clue says. It *might* mean coal, but that would mean the Bane."

Stevie made gestures of energetic digging. "The more —I dig—the warmer—I get." He paused. "Or it might mean something like a foxhole, the kind a soldier digs to keep warm in. No?" He saw that they were unimpressed.

They argued. Miggle's insistence that "warm" had to do with coal fell on deaf ears. Dub pointed out that the Bane hadn't been thought up a year ago, let alone a hundred. Except for a startled moment when Willy behaved as if there were something suspicious hiding in an up-

stream thicket, they wrangled. Not until Miggle, in a temper, announced with sarcastic dignity that there just might be an old mine tunnel or shaft around from the days when coal was mined underground, did Trish catch on, as Miggle had hoped she would right away.

"You mean that hole in the hill up back of the Dekanys'? Why didn't you say so?" She frowned. "You haven't ever gone in there, have you? We're not allowed."

Arthur was interested. "What kind of hole in the hill?"

Trish gave Miggle a sideways look full of suspicion. "An old mine shaft. It used to be all grown over, but Mr. Dekany cleared up the weeds. Sometimes he really digs coal in there. I don't think it goes in very far. Anyway he's got a wire door on it."

"A wire door?"

"You know," Miggle said quickly. "Like a Cyclone fence. Come on, it wouldn't hurt to *look*, would it? We can see in without opening the door. We wouldn't have to *go* in."

So they went. They straggled downhill past the dam, through the dusty Wood, and, by a short cut over a barbed-wire fence, across the Arthurs' upper pasture. They cut down through the orchard toward the strip of trees beyond the Dekany cottage.

At the bottom of the orchard Kit complained, "Ugh! My socks are full of burrs. Wait a minute."

But the others moved down through the tall grass under the apple trees and left her, sitting on a tree stump, to pull out the stickers that had worked through her thin socks to prick at her ankles.

Below, Miggle hissed a warning. "Keep behind the trees. Be careful Mrs. Dekany doesn't see you out her kitchen window."

Arthur and Stevie whistled at the size and darkness of the shaft. Their heads barely cleared the top of the entrance, but it was wide and the walls had at some time in the past been faced with rock. At a point about six feet into the hill, Mr. Dekany had closed the passage by fastening a heavy fence gate between the two stout old wooden supports to a heavy overhead beam. Beyond the gate the children could dimly make out a heavy pick and broad shovel leaning against a wheelbarrow. Opposite the wheelbarrow was a heavy wooden bin full of coal. Farther on was nothing but damp blackness. A cold, dank breeze breathed out from the hole.

"It's spooky. I don't like it." Trish shivered.

Stevie rocked back and forth on the balls of his feet. "Boy, oh boy! Wouldn't it be cool to explore in there? I wonder how far in it goes. It must go straight into the middle of the mountain." He frowned. "Do you suppose this treasure's clear under the mountain?"

Arthur was looking at the stonework. "Doesn't look very old," he observed, running a finger along the mortared joints. "But what about that beam? I bet it's been here forever." He reached overhead to feel along the ancient oak beam, but there was no gap between it and the earthen roof.

"If it's not outside the gate here," he said, "we'll have to tell Mr. Dekany. Will he think we're making the whole thing up, Mig?"

Miggle paled. "Oh, I don't think we ought to bother him," she blurted. "He . . . he can be awfully grumpy. And he wouldn't help. He would think we made it up so's to get into the mine."

She crossed her fingers guiltily. Mr. Dekany would spoil it all. He always said just what he thought, and she knew what he would think. Quickly, she moved close to the right-hand roof support and, pretending to inspect the gate hinges, slid her hand behind the heavy wooden prop.

"Oh! There's a space here between the pillar and the rocks. Uh, part way down it's like . . . like a little ledge. Um . . . just a minute."

Arthur, Stevie, and Trish crowded close.

"It feels kind of like . . ." Miggle pulled a grimy arm out, and in her palm lay a dusty flat packet like the others.

Trish wrinkled her nose and watched Miggle doubtfully as the packet was unwrapped. When Miggle acted so wide-eyed with surprise, it was safe to bet she was play-acting again. Arthur, in turn, noticed Trish's reaction and wondered what she was suspicious about. He watched Miggle with a new curiosity. No. He had discovered the old book himself. He put the doubt out of his mind.

"What does it say? Come on out into the light and read it."

Miggle handed it to him. By tilting it to catch the light he could make out:

Weſt into the Wood
Weſt over the riſe
From the boundery rock
Will find the prize.

"The boundary rock. Isn't that at the top of the orchard? Where the fence turns down the hill?" Stevie scuttled away and up the bank into the tall grass. "It is, isn't it? Come on, slowpokes."

Arthur followed and then Miggle, ignoring Trish's insistent tug at her shirttail.

A short way up the hill the pursuing Trish was stopped by a timid call from Kit, whom they had all forgotten. Trish turned back downhill while the others climbed on up the slope under a green roof hung with green apples. Here and there the apples clustered as thickly as globes on a chandelier, glowing softly with the first hint of a ripening red. The children did not notice. At the top of the orchard they followed the split-rail fence and its festoons of red raspberry brambles to the southwest boundary marker of Ridgebottom Farm. This was a huge mossy boulder into which long ago had been set a small brass plate reading:

S. W. Rdgbotm. Fm.

Using the rock as a stile, they crossed over into the Wood. In this part of the Wood, "west" was simply uphill, and the "rise" was clearly straight ahead. There was little undergrowth, and Arthur noticed that few of the trees were much more than saplings. The Wood here, like the worst part along the lower Run, was grayed with dust. Then they were scrambling to the crest of the slope, and he forgot dust, the Run, everything, for there were no trees there.

Miggle stared dumbly, and the boys drew back, wondering where they had gotten to. The Wood ended where they stood. To the right, an ash heap of a hill loomed up. It climbed steeply from the half-choked laurel bushes at their feet to hide the Ridge and half the sky. On the left the ground fell away sharply for about fifty feet, and from there dropped sheerly into the deepest part of the Bane. The bottom was hidden from view by the breast of the cliff. A bitter yellowish dust hung in the air.

"We've come wrong somehow," Miggle whispered. Then more firmly she said, "This can't be right. There's a wide strip of Wood and then the Barhatch Farm's upper meadow between us and the stripping. Let's go back to the rock."

"What good will that do?" Dub asked. "This must be that row of heaps we saw last night. Remember, the strip you said they must've dug up yesterday? And that blast at noon . . ."

"Oh, no!" Miggle at first would not believe it. It was

like the dream she sometimes had of walking down the highway through High Egg village and turning the corner toward Tipple only to find herself on a strange street in a strange town. When you turned back, the rest of High Egg was gone, too.

"Let's go back and try again," she said. Then she hesitated. The way today had been going, the boundary rock might be gone, too. That wouldn't be any odder than this. The Barhatch meadow and a wide swath of Wood had been wiped away.

The box and the beautiful key were gone as well, and the Elephants sang their unlovely song as they dug at the bones of the mountain.

Chapter Six

The box must be buried under a hill of rubble or deep in the Bane! Miggle felt somehow betrayed and would have given much to have someone to be furious at. She felt oddly hollow.

"For heck's sake, what's the matter, Mig?" Stevie asked. "Was there something special about the old trees and meadow? I mean, beside the treasure thing?"

It all had to come out. Arthur led Stevie and Miggle to a seat on a huge slab of rock apparently blown up from the slope below by the explosion. There, defiant and sniffling by turns, she told everything. The boys were one moment intrigued and bewildered the next. They cheered her by admiring the trail she had laid and in the next breath frankly called her a numbskull. Dub was disgusted. Stevie was more philosophical and therefore, from Miggle's point of view, more insulting. His shrug and elaborately casual turn of attention to the stones in his shoe seemed to say, "Girls! What else could you expect?"

"But I *know* it was something valuable," Miggle insisted.

"It *was*. It . . . it *felt* like a treasure: heavy and bright and . . . and smooth as satin."

"That's because Mr. Dekany polished it up for you," Arthur observed.

"Oh, you're horrid! You think I'm making it all up, don't you?" She snuffled up her nose so dramatically that Arthur dug out his handkerchief in alarm and thrust it at her.

"Thank you." She sniffled and blew gratefully.

"You might be making it up," Arthur agreed. "You made up all of today to hear you tell it, so why not?"

Stevie shook his head. "I don't think so. She wouldn't get so ugly and splotchy if it wasn't so. Come on, Mig. Show us what it looked like. The key, I mean."

Miggle glared but was glad of his curiosity. She bent for a shard of stone and used it as a crayon on the rock where they sat.

"I forget exactly what the handle end looked like," she said. What she drew was this:

"It looks like a piece of breakfast cereal stuck on the end there," Stevie observed.

Miggle swung her foot at him and missed. "You be quiet, Steve Griffith. Dub can see it's something special. Don't you think so, Dub?"

He shrugged unhappily. "It might've been. If it was, *you* deserve a swift kick."

"I guess so." She puzzled. "I don't know why, but it was like I was going two directions at once. I wanted so awfully for you to see it and help me find out about it. But somehow I got it in my head to hide it so it would be only mine; and then both things got sort of scrambled up in my dumb old head."

"You know what you do, Miggle?" Arthur looked at her sternly, pulling at his nose the way his father did when he was lecturing. "You want to map everything out, to see us go where you decide we ought to go. Heck, we've had lots more fun than today just . . . well, even chasing Merrylegs when she got loose. *Because* we didn't any of us know where such a silly horse would run next. No, that's not exactly what I mean. . . . Take when Stevie and I once were bashing around over Mishannock Run with quarterstaves: well, what fun would it have been if we did it like it was a stage play with every move spelled out, and then the 'wrong' person got knocked in first?"

He was not making himself clear; or rather he was not making the point he thought he was making. To Arthur, the excitement of games–and his imagination could make them very exciting–came from the not knowing, from the way you met the unexpected whatever-it-was around the next corner. In those terms the hunt had been real for the others but not for Miggle.

"You could always start all over again," said Miggle dubiously.

"In a play you can't. Not unless you want to on purpose to remind the audience it's all made up. It . . . it takes the edge off things if you know how they're going to come out. Not just in games–in everything." He was reminded of the awful math problems of the last week of school. "Well, almost everything."

"Yes, teacher," Miggle said sourly.

He puzzled. "Why *did* you make such a fancy fuddle of it? You sure didn't seem to be having much fun."

No, she hadn't. Suddenly, in her own way, she saw what

Dub meant. In a bright-edged flood of seeing, a dozen and more past disappointments came to mind, all looking very much alike. She laughed.

"I put *you* all in a box, in a terrarium, to watch you run around. Is that it? And I might never have told you. This time it was the Elephants who broke the box open."

As if on cue, the screech of heavy machinery took up again, close at hand. Stevie began to climb up the slope of the nearest mound to see what was going on, but as fast as he lifted one foot, the crumbling earth under the other slid down and left him no farther along than before. He drew back into the nearby trees to make ready for a long dash that would give him the momentum to reach the top. Arthur and Miggle next saw him in full retreat before a dust-foaming landslide that spilled from the monstrous gap-toothed mouth of a digging machine. The "head" of the crane, swaying on its cables, glowered over the mound, its mouth dribbling at the corners. It swung this way and that, searchingly, as if it could see. It clanked and yawned, baring awful teeth. Then it moved slowly along the heaped rubble toward the open side where the ground dropped away into the Bane a few yards from their rock.

Held breathless for a moment, Miggle squeaked.

Arthur, though he knew quite well that it could not see, that it was only dumping dirt from below, that it could not come close enough to "eat" them even accidentally, moved very quickly. He pulled Miggle from the rock so masterfully that one browned leg was scraped from the bottom of her cut-off jeans to the ankle. She found herself halfway down the Wood before she found her voice.

"Oo-ee!" she said faintly.

The boys walked bouncingly on the balls of their feet. They nodded at each other sympathetically, protectively, responsibly. But Miggle, once she had inspected the rock burn on her leg, shattered their growing fancy that they had snatched her, quite literally, from the jaws of death. With female persistence she returned to the interrupted conversation.

"Why aren't you still mad at me then?"

"Mad?" Dub wrinkled his brow. "About what, for Pete's sake?"

"About the *treasure*." She groaned. "And my fooling you all."

"Oh, that," he said vaguely. "I suppose the day wasn't a dead loss. There was the dead fish and the dead Wood and the mine into the mountain and all that. We did some good exploring no matter why we went."

He turned to her earnestly. "Why do you keep foaming on about your old treasure? Who cares about an old key anyhow? I *am* sorry your box got lost. But you don't give a hoot about a chunk of the mountain getting lost, do you? Now you see a pasture, now you don't. *There's* a real adventure. I mean, why couldn't we do something about it? Everybody just sort of stands around and watches and says, 'Dear-oh-dear-oh-dear.' "

They scrambled over the boundary rock into the old orchard and stepped Indian-file through the waist-high grass. Miggle was still weighing Dub's complaint skeptically when a voice came to them from above, on the right.

Trish and Kit sat in an apple tree, each astride a branch,

half hidden even to passers-by beneath. Kit was pale, freckles vivid in the white face below her untidy red hair. Trish was bursting with curiosity.

"Where've you been all this time? Did you find it? Where is it?" Her eyes glowed. "And did you see him? He followed you up the hill. Who d'you s'pose he is?"

"Who?" asked Arthur and Miggle and Stevie all at once.

"Why, that boy. The one you saw above the dam, I think. Kit saw him real close up, didn't you?" she said, turning to her cousin. "Tell them how funny he was."

"He wasn't funny," Kit answered in a small voice.

"Well then—queer, spooky. I don't see how a boy can be spooky. Anyhow, tell them."

Kit apparently had been truly frightened, but why she had been was not at all clear. While she had sat on an old apple-tree stump, pulling stickers from her socks and soothing the bramble scratches on her legs with a spitty finger, she had seen the boy pass. She had heard neither a footfall nor a rustle in the high grass, but suddenly he passed in front of her as smoothly and silently as a wisp of smoke. He had not seen her. She would have called out, she said, but her throat was very dry.

"And I was afraid I'd make him jump and he'd be angry."

"You ought to've made him jump," Stevie grumbled. "Who is he, anyhow? Sneaking around behind us like a barefooted Injun. Hey, maybe we can track him, Dub. Or maybe he's still behind us . . ." He darted a look over his shoulder.

"He followed you all back up from Mr. Dekany's orchard, too," said Trish.

"Did you see him, too? What did he look like?" asked Miggle. "It wasn't Sticky Barnes, was it? He walks like a junior hippopotamus." She pulled herself up onto a lower branch of the tree.

"No, I didn't see him," Trish answered, obviously disappointed that she had not seen for herself. "But Kit saw him clear as clear."

Heartened by the return of the older children and by their attention, Kit answered their questions, describing the boy with gestures and with a comical demonstration of her own frozen fright. The boy, whoever he was, had worn a plaid shirt and paint-stained too-big overalls, rolled up at the bottom like some old-fashioned picture of a farm boy whose mother bought things big enough for him to grow into. She had not been able to see whether he went barefoot or not.

"His hair was red. No, not like Stevie's and mine. More goldish. And he was real pale. And still. You know, like a face in a dream, all beautiful and scary." She hugged her arms as if a cold wind had passed. "And I couldn't really see, but I think . . . anyhow, for a minute I thought his eyes were like Willy's. They couldn't be, could they? That's why I got scared, I think."

Stevie pulled at his sister's foot. "Oh, come on down and stop showing off. People don't have eyes like that. You made it up. Unless he was a zombie." He leered horribly, and Kit pulled her feet up into the safety of the tree.

"Willy! Oh, glorious crud! Where *is* Willy?" Miggle smote her forehead.

They all looked around, vaguely, blankly.

"When did we see him last?" Arthur asked. "He wouldn't run away, would he?"

"No." Miggle was sure. "But his nose isn't very good. He might've lost us." She called.

They all called. And whistled. The strange boy was forgotten.

Trish squinted her eyes tight shut. "He was around all the time we were at Throne Rock. I remember. But not after, I think."

Miggle nodded. "Yes. He was sticking awfully close to me for a while. And after that, I don't know. Spit! D'you suppose he's lost up above the dam? Mother'll be upset if we leave him to find his own way. Sometimes he forgets to come until dark."

"Heck, I don't want to go all the way up there again," complained Stevie. "I'm hungry." He turned and scuffled through the downhill grass.

"I'll go," Dub offered. He wanted to poke around the Wood a bit more anyway.

No one argued with him. Stevie's mention of hunger brought Kit and Trish down out of the apple tree. Miggle hesitated for a moment. It was her dog and her fault for forgetting him, but her leg did sting, and she decided that she really ought to wash it off and put some Merthiolate on it. Besides, she was still irked at Arthur's lack of interest in the lost key. Its loss worried her, unaccountably, more than the thought of telling Mr. Dekany about losing the lovely box. She slid down and followed the others while Arthur climbed over the gate into the upper pasture and headed across it and into the lower Wood.

The stuffiness of the lower Wood had grown even worse, if that was possible, as the afternoon had deepened. Arthur cut across to the Run and followed it uphill, keeping to its wandering bank rather than to the straighter path. There was not even a johnny-craw to be seen in the pools. No lizards skittered among the rocks. At first the stream seemed clear enough, but as the ground rose toward the level of the Bane, Arthur saw first a touch of dimness in the water and then the yellowish veil he had noticed earlier. It could very easily have gone unnoted, for it was faint and almost invisible in the leafy shade. It was where the sun broke through the treetops to touch the water that it could be most clearly seen. In a rock pool he found another dead trout. It was only a fingerling some five inches long, its sides faintly marked with the promise of its rainbow.

Arthur flung it as far as he could through the trees. Not that rotten fish could do much harm to the water now.

"I bet every fish between here and the marsh is dead. Stinking Bane! Maybe Uncle Owen could write a letter to the Governor—or somebody." He spoke aloud, and the words hung in the thick air. As if in answer, the digging machines squealed and trumpeted deep in the hollow of the Bane.

"Stinking Elephants!" he proclaimed loudly.

Crossing over the dam, he was struck again by the greenness of the Wood above. It took the dead Wood to make you truly see the live one. Cool and clear, its shapes and shadows rushed upon his eyes. He turned to look down the slope of the dam to the point where the Run slid into the Wood below. Nothing moved. Leaves blurred into each other, and shadows were dirty smudges under a dusty roof. The deadness spread downhill in a widening swath from the road that ran out of the mouth of the Bane.

"The wind must come down through the Bane that

way," Arthur thought. First thing the next morning, he decided, he would get inside the Bane and have a look.

Meanwhile, there was Willy. Arthur called, cupping his hands to his mouth. "Hey, Willy? Willy . . . hi! Come, Willy! Terwilliger!"

No sound answered.

He put his fingers to his mouth and whistled ear-splittingly. Then again. And again. He paused, hearing no deep baying answer from Willy but a rushing, crackling, bounding sound that seemed to be coming down the long hill from the north. It was not like Willy not to give voice as he ran, and Arthur cautiously stayed in the open. His Uncle Owen had mentioned seeing a bear on the ridge by the Colwyn road. You weren't supposed to turn your back to a bear and run, but Arthur wasn't sure he could just stand and look at one if it barreled out of the Wood at him. He crossed his fingers.

Chapter Seven

It was almost a disappointment to see that it *was* only Willy who came running out of the woods, tearing joyously down the green funnel of the old road. He clattered across the stones along the water's edge to push against Arthur's knees and lick his hands with a generous tongue. He spun a dizzy circle around him and scrambled back across the spillway bridge. At the mouth of the old green road, he turned and waited, then stretched, bowing low on his front legs, panting, his rear end wriggling eagerly.

"Nutty dog." Arthur laughed. "What is it, boy? What do you want to go back up there for?" He approached, hand out to take the dog by the collar.

Willy misunderstood. He straightened, wheeled, and tore up the tree-arched road. He stopped far up at the bending of the way, stopped long enough to see that Arthur had not stirred, and barked. It was a deep, insistent bark. No clowning or smacking of lips to suggest a treat would lure him back.

"Oh, well," said Arthur. He looked up at the westering

sun. "It can't be past three o'clock. Or not much, anyway. Why not?"

He followed, and the greenwood closed behind him. If it had seemed alive an hour or two ago, it was far more vivid now. It was as if he had stepped out of the world and into a slower, clearer place. He thought it might be because there was no one to talk or listen to. The sounds of leaves, of leaf against twig, were so clear that he felt he might go tapping along the tree trunks and hear them ring like bells.

The rutted road bent to the right, away from the Run, and Willy sped with it. Some hundred yards beyond, where the tracks divided to the north and to the south, he stopped to sit and wait for Arthur.

"Where do you think you're going now?"

Willy's silver eyes watched to be sure that Arthur meant to follow, and then he trotted up the right-hand way, north along the skirts of the Ridge. Five or six times he waited and went on in this same fashion, climbing gradually until they reached a high lap of the hills.

The dog came to a fallen tree at the side of the overgrown roadway. It was half buried in waist-high ferns, and beyond was a clump of pale young tamaracks. Willy went over the log and through the trees. Arthur followed, protesting. He pushed the branches aside, treading on the soft needle carpet beneath. There he stopped in surprise.

Beyond, climbing up a gentle ravine between two high-shouldered hills, he saw a treeway walled with green damp-sheen trunks—beeches with arching ribs, hung with light and flickering blades of leaves. In back of them and above loomed old and shaggy hemlocks, tall and dark and still. The way was chandeliered with sap-stuck pale gold clusters of last year's leaves. It was perhaps an ancient road of the earliest loggers, lost since their time. It was carpeted with ankle-deep green that lay bruised and dark wherever Willy stepped. The light itself was green. There was no sunshine. No trees but beeches could live in that unbroken hemlock shade.

"Golly," Arthur breathed. "Old Miggle ought to see this. I bet she hasn't." But he was glad to be seeing it alone. The green light was almost like being under water.

Willy sat gently on his haunches, ready to move on, and grinned wetly. Tree holes and leaf carpet stirred with tiny groping paws. Willy's nose twitched with a brief curiosity, but he waited only for Arthur's absent-minded rub behind his ears and was off again.

The whole mountain must once have been like this, Arthur thought. Then settlers had come, intent on mastering the land, living *on* it rather than in and with it as the Indians had. He stepped into the treeway and walked on slowly, everything forgotten but this world of green gloom. Indians lurked behind his eyes with paint-smeared cheeks and bony pates.

"Hi, Willy!" He whistled.

Up ahead and beyond the greenway's edge, Willy crashed to a stiff-legged stop, one eye on a leafpile-like grouse with telltale beaded eyes and one ear cocked at his ringing name. For the grouse it was enough. It racketed through the silence, and Arthur, hard-eyed, lifted his arms to draw taut the string of an unseen bow and loose an imaginary arrow. The echo of the bird's lift blew away. Arthur raised his arms again to sight once more, and down the line of his thumbs' knuckles he saw a shadow move behind distant netted branches.

The dog far ahead edged out of the trees, paw by careful paw, and peered questioningly toward Arthur, who mouthed and nodded a "no" and thrust his palm out flatly for a sign to "stay." Willy did not move but laid his nose down on some scent and quivered with obedience. Probably a deer, Arthur thought. He moved quietly and quickly to where the dog sat. The feathery grass was thin and wet, and it soaked his shoes. The wet earth sucked at his heels.

The mark Willy showed him was no cloven print cutting deep into the damp earth, but what might have been a footprint much the size of his own. The grass was clearly bent, marked by such a shape, and lightly; and already it seemed to be springing back. When Arthur looked back at his own trail of dark smudges, he mistrusted Willy's nose. Still, it might be that boy. He dried his palms on his jeans nervously.

Willy begged, with an eager wriggling, to be released from "stay," and Arthur nodded. The dog turned uphill once more, leading him over the crest through a fall of sunshine and then off the road into the deep Wood. They had gone only a few yards when they were greeted by a clear voice from behind a screen of trees.

"I have been waiting for you."

The boy sat upon the ground inside a low and ragged circle of juniper, erect and pale. Here where there was no sunlight, his untidy hair seemed more gold than red. Despite his rough clothes, his hands were slim and smooth, milk-white as his face. His eyes were of a piercing blue.

"My name is Káolin. Thou . . . you are the one called Arthur?"

"Yes . . ." Arthur answered doubtfully. "Colin, you say?"

The other inclined his head. "It is near enough, and it comes to the same thing."

Arthur wondered if the boy might be funny in the head. Queer that he should be so at home on the mountain and no one knowing him or where he belonged. Arthur frowned and thrust his hands deep into his pockets. "You said you were waiting for me. You've been following after us all afternoon. What's the big idea?"

"It is the dog," Káolin answered, summoning Willy to his side. "I wish to . . . shall we say, I wish to have him. What will you take in his place? This?"

He held up a round rough stone the size of a large grapefruit.

"A rock? For Willy?" Arthur came close and grasped Willy's chain collar. "He isn't my dog, but even if he were, I sure wouldn't swap him for an old rock."

Silently, the boy moved from the rock he sat upon and tapped the round stone sharply upon it. It split into two halves, and in each was cupped a meat brighter than fruit—a heart of amethyst crystals.

Arthur was held despite his distrust. "It . . . it's a geode, isn't it? I've never seen one outside of a museum."

Touching it, he met the other's eyes and knew what Kit had meant. This . . . Colin's attention had withdrawn from him, and the blue eyes had paled almost to silver. Arthur felt an uneasy, unreasoning fear. He found himself thinking, "I hate him." Astonished and ashamed, he put the thought out of his mind.

"The dog belongs to whom then?"

"To my cousin Margaret."

"The oldest of the girls? Why can you not then give the jewel to her?"

"Well, because. Because he's hers, and I don't think she'd want to give him away for anything. It's a super geode, though," he added weakly. "And Miggle does collect rocks."

He pulled at Willy, who looked from one to the other, confused. Then, despite himself, Arthur blurted rudely, "Why do you want him? Because of his eyes?"

The blue gaze darkened and held his. "In part. But not, I think, for the reason which is in your mind. Among my people there is a saying—an old song—about a particolored dog with silver eyes: that such a one coming upon a mountain with a dark boy will. . . . But no mind. If it is only with . . . if it is only through a girl that he may come to us, he is not the dog of the old rhyme. At least I do not think it can be understood so, and I am sorry to have brought you so far."

He smiled, looking not in the least disappointed.

"Oh, that's O.K." Arthur was relieved but bewildered. What sort of reason for wanting a dog was that? You might as well go around looking for jumbucks because you liked to sing "Waltzing Matilda." Curiosity pulled at him.

"That's O.K.," he repeated lamely. "Well, um . . . I guess we'd better get going. My Aunt Vi will be wondering where we've got to." He pulled at Willy.

"And you are hungry." There was a laugh behind the blue eyes, and Káolin seemed at once older and less frightening. Arthur doubted whether that made sense, but it was so.

"Yes," he answered. "I guess I am. If I don't hurry, it'll be too late for me to get anything to eat before suppertime."

"Then will you come with me to my home?" Káolin gestured toward the greenway and beyond the crest of the ravine it climbed. "There will be cakes and something cool and sweet to drink, if naught else. Your long walk home will be the shorter for a rest and some small refreshment."

Curiosity won. The boy's speech was oddly stiff, and Arthur wondered where there could be any house up on the Ridge top, where there was no road. Being assured that it was not far, he followed, with Willy close at his heels. He was forced to stretch his stride as Káolin–or Colin–moved swiftly beneath the hemlocks to join the greenway where the long hill crested. The road there bent gently down, and they came into a wide grassy clearing where the sunshine slanted in to warm the air and wash the greens with gold.

Káolin led the way across the small meadow to a narrow path among wide oak trees on its western rim. This seemed little more than a deer trail, narrow and winding, bending with the slope, turning back upon itself, but yet steadily moving upward. Arthur found his breath coming harder and felt Willy panting damply just behind his knees.

At last, pausing by what seemed a hedge, a wall, of laurel, Káolin stood waiting for them. Arthur and the dog came up to him, breathless.

"It is beyond," he said, showing Arthur a gap in the close-woven wall of laurel.

On the other side Arthur saw that they had come to another small meadow. Laurel-rimmed and cupped below the blue sky by ringing trees on three sides, it was walled on the fourth by a sheer rock face that stretched some thirty yards up a steep slope. Arthur thought he might be near the summit of the Ridge, but the winding path had so muddled his sense of direction that he could not be sure.

Opposite, against the rock wall and shadowed from the afternoon sun by the hill above, stood a house of stone, little more than a lean-to against the hill behind. They moved toward it. Arthur began to worry whether he ought to stay for the offered refreshment. There might not be enough. And it was such an odd-looking place. The boy's mother might offer him some awful thing like watercress sandwiches or acorn bread and dandelion wine. He had heard of such things, and this looked like just such a place—a place where orange marmalade and English muffins and sugar cookies had not yet reached. But the door had swung open to Káolin's touch, and it was too late to make excuses without being rude.

Scarcely a step beyond the first, a second door opened inward, and Arthur found himself in a large room dimly lit by candles. Except for a large open fireplace and two narrow windows that looked out upon the meadow, the walls were covered with hangings of some heavy stuff. There were chairs of ash and walnut, two large maple cupboards, and before the fireplace stood a long table made with trestles and boards. It was set with pitchers of frothy milk and of buttermilk, with basins of what might have been pudding, with loaves and butter and small flat cakes, and with tall flagons cold and wet as if they had been chilling in a mountain spring.

"This is Arthur, of whom we have spoken," Káolin

said, and to Arthur it sounded as if these people had wanted to meet *him*, not the dog. Willy had been forgotten.

"And these are my mother Maelin and my mother's mother Rhelemon," said Káolin.

A woman in a blackbird-colored cloak sat by the cold hearth, and one who seemed younger stood by the table, setting out spoons and goblets. Her dress was green, and her petticoat hung below, blue as a peacock's breast. Her hair was tied back with a bit of green lace, and she wore on her breast a blue stone. She was no taller than her son.

"You are welcome, Arthur," she said. "It is a good name you bear. I trust you bear as good an appetite and that our table tempts you? We were about to have something to stave off thoughts of supper. Will you have some buttered oatcakes and a drink of *glasdur?* Or there is fresh milk if you like."

"Yes, thank you. Milk, I mean, not . . . the other." He did not know whether *glasdur* meant the stuff in the chilled flagons or the buttermilk, and he didn't like buttermilk. It was all even odder than watercress sandwiches. The oatcakes were spread thick with butter, but he drew back his hand. He had never eaten oatcakes, and the other foods were equally unfamiliar. The milk was cool. The goblet from which he drank was old and fashioned of a dull metal paler than pewter.

Arthur tried hard to think of something polite to say, for no one spoke. They watched him, kindly (he thought), but did not take food or drink themselves. The woman by the hearth let fall the hood of her cloak, and Arthur saw that, though her hair was silver, her face was smooth and fair as a girl's. Alarmed, he set the goblet down carefully.

"Will you play a game?"

A man's voice, richer but of the same high clearness as Káolin's, startled Arthur from the shadows by the window to his right. A small table inlaid with chessboard squares stood beneath the window, and the speaker motioned for him to come nearer. He bowed slightly without rising from his chair and gestured for Arthur to sit opposite him.

"Káolin is my son. I am called Durwen," he announced. "I have played so long and often with these and other members of my household that I can foresee their plotting five moves ahead. Do you play? I should be glad of a new partner."

"I'm not very good," Arthur objected, wondering at the oddness of this family. He picked up one of the pieces and turned it over in his hand.

"Which piece is this? The pawn?"

It was formed more like a large counter for checkers or backgammon and was shaped from ivory with carven scrollwork and richly colored insets of blue and red of some hard material. He picked up other pieces and found them all strange. One might have been a tree; another was wound about with lacing serpents.

"Pawn?" Durwen seemed puzzled. He leaned forward over the table. "Ah, I see. No, no, this is not chess. Will you not play at *fidchell* then?"

"*Fidchell?*" Arthur returned the counters to the table. For the first time he saw Durwen clearly, and his first fear returned. The faintly silvered red-gold hair was caught back behind his ears and hung almost to the collar of a furred gown of rough blue cloth. His face was of a frightening fairness. Kit's words, "Like a face in a dream, all beautiful and scary," whispered in Arthur's ear. He scraped his chair back and excused himself hastily to everyone.

"It'll be suppertime before I get home to Ridgebottom. Thanks . . . thanks a lot for the milk. Good-by, Mrs.—er, ma'am. Colin?" He looked around in confusion. "Where's Willy?" What if the dog had been stolen away?

"The dog waits outside." Káolin spoke, not moving.

Arthur went to the door. Soft words spoken behind him half formed themselves in his mind. Only later did he piece them together.

"We must speak no more of it, Káolin," he seemed to have heard. "This cannot be the boy. Not even if the digging on the mountain goes deeper can we take such a chance. We are too many. Go now; see him to his road."

Willy and Arthur had plunged down the long beech-arched greenway at full tilt, thrusting through the tamaracks and scrambling over the fallen log to stand breathless in the more familiar roadway. They were still almost a mile north of the dam. Arthur was so intent upon getting home and indoors that he noticed nothing all the downhill way until the last path met the Ridgebottom Farm fence. The final stretch across the meadows was taken at a tired foot-dragging pace.

"Phew! Am I late?" He banged the sun-porch door shut.

Stevie, the girls, and Aunt Vi sat at the sun-porch table.

"My heavens, Arthur! Did you run all the way? Willy

can be such a nuisance wandering off like that. I hope he hadn't gone very far. Here, I was just about to fill the glasses. You're just in time. Iced tea or lemonade?"

"Iced tea, please." He looked at the bowl of bananas and plate of cookies. "Have you finished supper then? Where's Uncle Owen?"

Trish and Kit looked at each other. Miggle and Stevie stared.

"What on earth do you mean, dear?" Mrs. Arthur wrinkled her brow. "It's only three-thirty. We're having teatime a bit early. And what is that dirty thing? A rock?"

Outside, the sun rode high in the sky, and in his hands he held the geode.

Chapter Eight

"I don't believe it," Miggle was still saying at breakfast time the next morning. "If this Colin wanted to swap an amethyst geode for Willy, why'd he give it to you anyway when you wouldn't trade? And I think you're making it up about how far you went and all that."

They had the Geological Survey map spread out on the dining-room table, but it told no more than it had the evening before, when Mr. Arthur had pointed out that there was no such ravine and no such steep rock wall as Dub had seen at the back of the stone house, not for miles along the Ridge.

As for the folk he had met there, he had hemmed and hawed. Their vividness had vanished, or in daylight and on home ground he had chosen to disbelieve it. His description of the dark room, the fireplace furnished with tripods, tongs, and spits, and the food he had been offered—all these had seemed to his aunt no more than what she expected hill folk might have. It was odd, though, to hear of any so far north; and to judge from Arthur's tale, odder yet that they should have lived so long upon the Ridge unnoticed. Yet, in the southern mountains there had once been a folk so long shut off from the outside world that, when found, they still spoke the language of the days of the first Queen Elizabeth. Arthur was interested and relieved at hearing such a sensible explanation.

This morning his attention was once more on the Bane, and he pulled the map out from under the toaster and sugar bowl to fold it into a smaller rectangle.

"Why do you have to keep fussing about the old geode?" he complained. "How do I know why he gave it away? Maybe because I said you collected rocks. I gave you the best half, didn't I? And it's no good trying to get me up there again. I didn't like that Colin. Besides, I've got more important things on my mind."

With a pencil he marked a point on the map below the dam where the road branched south into the Bane. "We'll go in that way," he indicated. "And I'll try to mark on here just how big a piece of the mountain they've ripped up."

"Good idea," remarked his Uncle Owen, looking up from his bacon and eggs and Kennington *Star-News*. "Tell you what, Arthur. Do you remember what I showed you last night about how to read the contour markings and to line up landmarks on that kind of map? If you make a careful job of it, I'll write that letter to the Governor you suggested and put in a copy of your map. It may not do any good, but it's worth a try."

"Are you going to go into Kennington today, Owen?" Mrs. Arthur buttered a piece of toast for Rover. "Or will Rob Padgett have had time to trace that deed yet?"

Mr. Arthur sighed and folded his napkin. "No. He won't be able to get at the Court House records until Monday. If he finds what he's afraid of, we're going to get together all the information we need to apply for a court order the minute Minshew looks cross-eyed at Ridgebottom Farm. It's a blasted nuisance! No, I think I'll do that job on the chicken-coop roof today. The tar paper's in the barn, isn't it? And where are my old overalls —the ones I use to paint in?"

Mr. Padgett's news of the day before was at the bottom of Mr. Arthur's gloom and his determination to do a job he had been putting off for months. The lawyer had found that in case after case the farmers in the path of the Bane had not wanted to sell their land—at any price. Yet each had ended in selling for a price less than the land was worth. A telephone conversation with Farmer Barhatch—who had only the day before watched, with tears in his eyes, his lovely northwest meadow disappear into the Bane—revealed what had happened to them all. Years ago—in Mr. Barhatch's case, as in some others, back in the days of his grandfather—the mineral rights to the farm had been sold to small mining companies. This meant that all minerals and coal that lay beneath the ground belonged to the mining company that bought the rights. This company had the further right to build any roads or make any "improvements" on the surface that were needed to get the coal out. One such mine had been the old drift mine that tunneled straight back into the mountain from the bottom of the Dekanys' orchard. Others had been deep shafts higher in the Wood, long ago played out and the upper levels filled in and covered over so that neither people nor animals could fall in. The seam of coal had grown too thin to pay for the sinking of more shafts and the digging of more galleries. Grass had covered the ties where the narrow railway tracks had lain. Except when, occasionally, some boy found a railway spike large and square and fashioned by hand, the mines were completely forgotten.

There was another exception, as it turned out: the Minshews. Mr. Clifford Minshew's father, Orval, had very quietly bought up for next to nothing these rights from each of the four or five small companies as they closed up their mines. And then he waited. Or forgot. His son remembered; and one day his son had the heavy machinery for getting at the wide thin seam by stripping down from the surface.

"Now I'm not a greedy man," he had said to Farmer Barhatch. "I've the right to take the road to the coal, and if that means a road a hundred and fifty feet deep, legally I still don't owe you a penny. But I know you lose the use of a pasture, and I feel real bad about that. Tell you what." He had scratched his plump chin. "I'll give you a thousand dollars and take the rock piles my machines will leave off your hands. The land'll be no good to you. Least I can do!" And he had patted his large stomach.

"Do you no good to take it to court," he had added shrewdly. "Those old deeds are all in order. Just cost you a lot of lawyer's fees, and there'd be no thousand bucks. Only a heap of shale and sandstone that won't grow good grass for a hundred years."

Mr. Arthur was in a better position than the farmers to risk the lawyer's fees. If that shallow seam of coal was wide enough to dip under Ridgebottom Farm, no groaning, squalling Elephant was going to come chewing at it. There was still a chance, of course, that the Minshew Coal Company would have no claim to it. Mr. Padgett was to examine the old Ample and Hinks deeds, as well as the present one, to be doubly sure of how things stood.

In the meantime, Mr. Arthur could hammer away at the chicken-coop roof clad in old golf shorts and an ancient shirt. With the breakfast dishes washed and dried, everyone went off in different directions: Trish and Kit to feed the chickens and collect the warm brown eggs, Morton (and his mother) to feed the dogs, and Miggle and Arthur to clean out Duke's and Bobble's and Merrylegs' stalls in the barn. Stevie helped brush the horses and carried water from the spring pond for the chickens. The air was already moist and uncomfortably warm. The horses trotted through the gate into the lower meadow and rolled there in the grass, hoofs up, wriggling like puppies. They still needed exercise badly. "Maybe when it's not so hot, we can go riding," Miggle said, closing the gate. Today there was the Bane.

The younger girls did not care much for the idea of exploring the Bane. "It's too dusty and dirty," was Trish's excuse. Instead, they decided to begin a patchwork quilt and shortly had bright snippets and squares of cloth from the scrap box littered over the sun-porch table. Miggle and the boys, equipped with canteens, a picnic lunch in a basket, and a pink and green parasol, set off down the road. Willy was invited to follow and came gladly.

"Come on; put that thing down, Mig," Stevie grumbled. "At least until we're off the road. You look like a nut. It's not that hot yet, anyway."

Miggle, who was in a high good humor, collapsed the offending parasol and tucked it under her arm.

"Was the man short, too? Hey, Dub!" She poked his arm with the parasol. "Put the old map away. I want to know. Was he short, too?"

Arthur frowned at being distracted; or rather, he frowned at the question, which he had heard and ignored.

"Who? Was who short?"

"You know who I mean, Arthur Arthur. That Durward or whatever his name was. Colin's father. What was their last name?"

Arthur shrugged. "They didn't say. Who cares anyway."

"*I* do." She bounced along, her braids flapping. "I've got an idea. About them, I mean. Why've you got to be such a lemon? *Was* he short?"

"How am I supposed to know? He was sitting down the whole time. Maybe he was. I don't know."

Miggle eyed him shrewdly. "What did they look like? You remembered about their furniture and stuff, but you kept steering away from telling Mother and Daddy what they looked like, their clothes and all that."

"They didn't ask me. Only girls notice that kind of stuff, anyway."

"Well, you'd notice if they wore ordinary farm clothes or plain things like the Amish. Or bird feathers," she added, watching him closely.

"*Bird* feathers!" Stevie hooted.

Arthur grinned. "You *are* loony this morning. No, none of them were wearing bird feathers. That Colin had on an old plaid shirt with the sleeves cut off short. And dirty overalls. His father's, I guess. They were rolled up at the bottom and so big that he had them tied around the middle with a string." As he spoke, a frown began to wrinkle his forehead. The image of Durwen in overalls was all wrong.

"And the others?" asked Miggle.

"First you tell me why you're so curious." He kicked at a rock. "What's this screwy idea you've got?"

"I won't tell," she insisted, "until you tell me if they all looked like farmers or hillbillies or whatever. Or was it only Colin?"

"No . . . they didn't. So what?"

"Because." She turned triumphantly, walking backwards as she faced Arthur and Stevie. "Because I bet it was Daddy's shirt and overalls, and he stole them. Or anyway swapped something for them. When I went out to the garage after breakfast this morning, I couldn't find Daddy's painting clothes for him, but I did find this hanging on their hook."

Reaching into a pocket, she drew out a long blue ribbon and fluttered it in the air. "It's a belt, I think. Anyway it's strong enough to be one. But feel how light it is. Here, look."

Willy pushed close, trying to smell it, but she held it high.

Reluctantly, Arthur accepted it. It was a bit more than an inch wide and was woven from some lustrous thread not unlike silk, yet lighter and softer to the touch. What was most unusual was the shifting, shimmering color and the design, patterned after the eye of a peacock's feather, which was repeated every ten inches or so along its length. Arthur looked at it closely. The design was fashioned of small overlapping tips of birds' feathers woven directly into the fabric: feathers of several shades of blue, green, warm dove gray, and the sheeny blue-black of a crow's wing. He remembered the blackbird-colored cloak of Rhelemon who sat by the cold hearth in the dark house.

"Could be that Colin left it," he admitted grudgingly. He passed the ribbon to Stevie. "But what does that prove? It wasn't exactly stealing if he left something better than what he took. And he did give me an amethyst geode that's bigger than any they've got in the Science Museum in Poole *or* up in Pittsburgh."

"No, I didn't mean that." Miggle sobered. "I just meant they . . . they're *different*. We've missed lots of things, ever since winter. Not before that that I can think of. You know, funny things: my new school notebooks I left on the sun porch, odds and ends of old clothes, even a sack of old road maps Daddy was going to throw out. Every time, though, we found something: an old Indian arrowhead or a green stone, or a bunch of flowers. Kind of like a pack rat does. And food, too, sometimes. Like the milk yesterday. Remember the jar full of fresh mint in the 'fridge?"

"Aw, come on, Mig! Clear inside the house?"

"Well, your old Colin could have done it without Mother hearing a thing down there in the basement. I think I'll ask him if I see him." She swung the picnic basket. "You know, they might just be awfully poor, and maybe we could help. Or they might be . . ."

"Might be what?" Arthur asked automatically. His mind was elsewhere, recalling Durwen's whispered words: "This cannot be the boy. Not even if the digging on the mountain goes deeper can we take such a chance. We are too many. . . ." The Bane. They might be in dread of it, too, and his fear of their strangeness had closed his ears.

"Might be what?" he repeated, remembering the strange fairness of Maelin in her green gown.

"Oh, nothing." Miggle grinned mischievously, throwing off her seriousness. "Just . . . different. What did you think I meant?" She retrieved the ribbon and tied it around her waist. "Come on! I'll race you both to the Bane!"

They climbed the last few yards to the foot of the dusty road that bent into the Bane and stood a moment, breathless from running. Above, they could see the crazy-tilted bulldozed trees and steeple-high heaps of cindery earth.

"You can go ahead and do your old map if you want to," said Miggle. "I'm going to look for my walnut box."

"In *there?* It's probably under a million tons of this crud." Stevie ground a lump of the soft shale beneath his heel.

"I know. But it won't hurt to look."

Arthur, bending to watch something by the roadside, moved upwards toward the foot of the nearest yellow-brown ridge of raw earth and rock. From under its skirts seeped a thin trickle of bitter yellow water. It slipped downhill through the sparse growth of grass and weeds to make its sluggish way across the trucking road at a point where the ruts were deep and crisscrossed. He touched the water and brought his fingers to his mouth. He spat.

"Pew! I knew it," he crowed. "Look, Steve. This bitter water. Just smell it. That's what's been killing the trout. If we could only get the Game Warden or somebody up here to test this stuff and the water in the Run!"

"Maybe the man from the State Fish Hatchery at Kittamaugy," Miggle suggested. "They put more than a thousand little trout in the Run just this spring, up above the dam somewhere."

The children made their way over the brow of the road to look down into the long V-shaped slash that led to the deepest reaches of the Bane. The road bent downward, keeping to the bottom of the canyon valley until it divided, branching in a Y shape to the right and left. South beyond the forking of the valley and above to the west, mountainous heaps piled against each other in long uneven rows: cruelly pointed teeth threatening to tear away the Wood and fields. Willy drew close to Miggle and pushed, as if to turn her back. He whimpered.

Chapter Nine

"Let's go down there and see how deep it goes." Arthur pointed down the road.

For half an hour they prowled the Bane together, each reluctant to leave the others. Miggle and Stevie listened while Arthur puzzled over ways to halt Mr. Minshew's greedy Elephants. They could write all the letters in the world, he said, and even if anybody stopped to listen to you, there were always investigations and endless arguments before anybody up and *did* anything. When people got older, they acted as if they thought talking was doing.

When Miggle asked what Arthur meant by "doing," he had to think for a minute.

"Well, sabotage maybe. Maybe siphoning all the diesel oil out of the Elephants."

"Ugh!" Stevie made a face at the thought. "Gasoline's bad enough. Pop once let me get some out of our car for the lawnmower. Besides, they'd just get more."

Arthur agreed that they would but protested that it was time that was needed and that an hour or two's delay was better than nothing. Miggle wondered whether it might not be better to scare away the drivers of the Elephants, to make everybody think the hill was haunted.

"Like in a story I read once," she explained, "where the kids all got dressed up in sheets and rode around on moonlight nights on their ponies, scaring away the people who camped in their bird sanctuary and left garbage all over the place. I think it was a bird sanctuary. Anyway, one of us could fix up like a headless horseman, all in white, and ride down the Bane on Merrylegs. She looks like a ghost horse in the moonlight, all white and shiny."

Arthur looked interested. "You can do some real neat things with phosphorescent paint on white stuff—make it look like bones shining through."

"But they've got those big old floodlights on all night," Stevie objected.

They went on a while in silence, coming at length to the dividing of the steep valley into a deeper canyon on the left and a long ravine climbing upward on the right. Far down the lower road, at its end, a small lake of black water filled the deepest part of the chasm. Beyond it, as far as they could see, the naked heaps humped off to the south. The road stopped short of the black water, and on the other three sides the slopes plunged steeply to the water's edge, affording no way around the lake and over the heaped hills beyond. High above to the west—beyond the desolation spreading out from the upper road—a few treetops could be seen through the shimmering air.

The heat was oppressive. The sun was still an hour from noon, but the bare slopes caught the sun's rays, reflecting and intensifying the heat. There was no shade.

"Let's try up that way." Arthur pointed to the upper road. "We can find out how far up the Ridge they've gotten south of the dam. And if I can get clear up on top, I ought to be able to see enough to mark the boundaries out on this map. We ought to stick together."

"O.K., but I want to take a look at that lake afterwards," said Stevie, agreeably taking a turn at carrying the lunch basket.

Miggle followed. From the high ground perhaps she could see where Mr. Barhatch's wood and meadow had been ripped away. There was, she knew, little likelihood that she would ever see her box and the key again, but —as she told herself—it would not hurt to look.

The road crested on a broad high shoulder where the earthen hills had been scraped level to make a place for the large bulldozers and earth-moving machines, a safe place where blasts could not shake loose avalanches of dirt to tumble down over them. Farther on, an untidy attempt at filling in the small ravines along the highest reaches of the desolation made it possible for the rough road to hump on southward, where it eventually came out onto the proper road where it joined Highway 32. There, scraggly heaps thinly crowned with rank grasses and bordered with thistles showed how little thirty years had done to heal an earlier and short-lived attempt at strip mining in the area.

"Here, you kids! Get away from them machines!"

The rough voice startled them, and they could not for a moment see where it had come from. Then a figure moved down the slope toward them. He had apparently been sitting at the top, his dark clothing unseen against the far fringe of treetops. He held a shotgun loosely in the crook of his arm, the barrel pointing groundwards.

"Go on, clear off! We don't want nobody nosin' around

them machines." He waved them back the way they had come.

The children moved reluctantly. Arthur hung behind, trying to guess at the distances across and down the length of the stripping. His map he thrust inside his shirt so that the man with the shotgun would not think that they were spying. It could be marked later.

"I'm going down the other way and have a look at that lake," Stevie called.

Willy had disappeared at the first sound of the strange voice.

Miggle dawdled, waiting for Arthur, who moved nonchalantly, hands in pockets, looking this way and that.

"Hurry up!" she hissed. "He's watching you."

The dark figure stood on the brow of the road behind them until they reached the meeting of the roads far below, and then he disappeared.

"Oh, he was horrid!"

Arthur breathed more easily, too. "Golly, did you ever see anyone so mean-looking? That flat ugly face and wee little eyes."

"He looked like he really would have shot at us. Do you think he would?"

"No . . . but I sure wouldn't want to go spooking around up here at night." He wiped his damp brow on his forearm.

"I wonder why he's here anyway." Miggle frowned. "I've never seen anybody up here on a Saturday before."

"Maybe they *are* afraid somebody will put sand in their old fuel tanks or something. What do you bet somebody has been trying to sabotage them?"

"Mm, hm." Miggle scanned the slopes at the mouth of the lower road. Where did you start to look when you had lost a needle in a haystack? "There must be more than us who would like to," she agreed.

She was interrupted by the soft hiss of cascading earth and Willy's excited bark. Down the long steep side of the canyon behind them, straight down from the roadless maze of mounds high to the west, the boy Káolin ran on feather-light feet. Behind his easy leaping descent came Terwilliger, cartwheeling wildly in a frantic cloud of legs and ears, dust and clods of earth. He crashed with a resounding thump.

Miggle hesitated, torn between curiosity and Willy's yelps. Then to Arthur she cried, "Quick! See if he's broken anything, and then come on."

She bounded after Káolin, running full tilt down the dusty road. Her long braids and the ribbon of blue belt fluttered behind.

Káolin was far ahead at the farthermost end of the road, bending over something at the edge of the dark water. Miggle's heart gave a thumping turn. Stevie had come down this way. He hadn't waited for them.

She ran like the wind, skimming over the stones, raising a trail of dust that hovered over the road behind. Red-faced and frightened, she came to a breathless stop beside Káolin, who sat some yards from the water with his arm around a shivering, gulping Stevie.

"What's the matter? Did he fall in? Is–is he O.K.?" The words tumbled over each other.

"You may thank the dog that he is," Káolin replied sternly. "This is no place for those who would forget simple caution. Neither is it a place for children to play unless they know that there is no fast line between a simple game and what cannot be undone. There is waste and danger in this place, and it needs no drowning to make it evil." He spoke bitterly.

"But we . . . we weren't playing. We were exploring. We were looking for . . ."

"For you it is the same, call it what you will." He drew a soft white kerchief from inside his shirt and gently wiped Stevie's face. "This one had been drawn into the water by its pull upon the soft and shifting earth, much as the sand in an hourglass is sucked down. Only his feet and ankles were to be seen when I reached the verge." He dried Stevie's hair.

Stevie sneezed. "It—it was so cold I c-couldn't move. I could see and—and think, but it was so c-cold my bones hurt, and I couldn't move."

"Come." Káolin beckoned to Miggle. "Let us take this wet shirt off. He will be warmer without its chill against his skin. Both he and it will soon be dry in this heat."

"What's going on? What happened?"

Arthur hurried toward them. He had been carrying Willy, but when he caught sight of his cousin's white face and ruffled hair, he dropped the dog without ceremony and ran. It was clear from the wet clothes what had happened. He forgot his mistrust of Káolin in his concern for Stevie, whose paleness was made more startling by the warmth of his wild red hair.

"Golly, even your freckles are pale. You O.K.?"

"S-sure." Stevie sneezed again.

"What can I do?" Arthur turned instinctively to Káolin.

"It will help if you will take the other side and do as I do. Rub his arm and shoulder briskly. The hand and fingers, too. He is as cold as any fish. Yes, that is the way."

Some moments later, when Stevie had begun to regain his color, Káolin looked over his shoulder and saw Willy picking his way to them gingerly. He limped on his right hind leg.

"Ah, the dog has lamed himself. I will have a look in

a moment. He is *Mailcûn* indeed, a princely hound, the best of dogs."

Willy grinned foolishly as if he understood. He limped to Miggle's side and pushed his cold nose against the back of her knee. Worried, she moved her hand gently down the leg, feeling along the bone.

"It isn't broken. He must've bruised it. Or sprained it maybe. He looked like a pinwheel coming down that hill."

"These shifting hills are not to be trusted," Káolin said. "The wild animals have long had the wit to keep to the Wood and well away from these uncertain mazes." Rising, he helped Stevie to his feet. "Now that you are free of the chill of the Black Lake, tell me how it drew you within its reach. There are reasons why I must know, though it may seem of little weight to you."

Miggle watched and listened to Káolin with dawning wonder. Without thought the three children had accepted his bidding, doing it without question. He was no boy. She saw in his smooth face and fair blue eyes something without age, a fairness at once ancient and young. She had half thought that he might be like this; or rather, she had spun such a tale in her head, wishing it true. She fingered the ribbon at her waist and did not dare to speak for fear that at the touch of a word this Káolin would blur before her eyes into the scrawny mountain boy Arthur had so desperately wanted him to be.

"I just wanted to have a look at it," said Stevie, puzzled. "You know–to see if it was just a big puddle or maybe a hole from one of those big explosions. Then there was this dark round thing underwater a little ways. I thought it might be Miggle's box, so I lay down flat to be safe and tried to fish it out. It was only a rock, though. I didn't know I was sliding in until I opened my eyes underwater. Everything was sliding. And it was steep."

He looked around excitedly. "Guess what I did see down there in the shadows! A big bulldozer! I bet that's why that guard's up there. I bet somebody pushed it in."

Káolin frowned. "No, it was left here near the water and forgotten until after the pond had taken it. The men here may think it stolen. But tell me: was it moving downward?"

"Yes. Everything was. I don't understand. How could there be a hole that deep? It must be deeper than it is wide across."

Káolin nodded. "I fear so. And that is why it seems so black. Yet to attempt explaining what I do not myself fully understand would be folly. Perhaps Durwen could tell you more of this."

He touched Stevie's arm. "Do not worry. You have not done ill. Your curiosity drew you, and you could not know your peril. Indeed, I am thankful that the peril was no more." He would explain himself no further and withdrew as if to leave them.

"Colin?"

Arthur had been silent for a long while, but now he spoke, his eyes fixed stubbornly on his dusty shoes.

"It was my fault. I kind of felt something funny about this whole Bane, but I put it out of my head. We ought to have stuck together. Anyhow, what I mean is . . . thanks for helping." His eyes met Káolin's for an instant and fell again.

"There are many things your heart puts in your head

which you thrust away." Káolin smiled grimly. "It is a habit men learn too soon and hold to, often to their loss. Yet I also may be mistaken in this matter. I spoke harshly a while ago of the waste and danger which speak of a larger evil in this place, where it seemed you spun out a tale to play with on an empty day. But your cousin Margaret has protested that you had some purpose here. In my concern for the boy I did not listen. I will listen now, for we may yet have reason to be friends."

"You *ought* to know what we were doing," Arthur answered, still mistrustfully. "You've been padding around behind us, eavesdropping, since yesterday, haven't you?"

"I have been watching you, yes; but I have heard little." He paused, as if seeking the best way to explain. "We have lived since winter in fear of what ruin this mining might bring upon the mountain, and we had reason to believe that you might be of help, unlikely as that may have seemed. But you have not answered *me*. Have you a purpose here beyond amusement? If so, I would hear it."

Arthur, caught by Káolin's concern, told of his own and his uncle's fears for the farm and the Ridge. He told of the map.

"Good." Káolin smiled. "Your heart and mind can still work together to a good end. Yet you fear us. Why?"

"I don't know." Arthur spoke haltingly. "Because . . . well, because you seemed to want me to do or be something, and I didn't know what. It was like you were all *watching* what I was thinking. I just wanted to get out. Why pick on me?"

"It has to do with the dog, as I told you. In the springtime when first he saw it, Durwen recalled to us a dark rhyme in the ancient tongue of our people which spoke of a dark-haired boy and a parti-colored dog with silver eyes who would be an omen of our freedom. The song said only 'freedom,' not from what we were to be freed. Yet Durwen and Túdual and some others thought that if it spoke of you, it might also speak of the Bane, as you have named it. The name suits well."

Arthur flushed, remembering. "But Durwen said I wasn't the one. Why was that?"

Káolin looked up the road uneasily. "We should not linger here," he murmured. Then turning again to Arthur he said, "I will take a chance, as chance has brought me to you this morning. Will the three of you—and the dog—come with me? It would be better that Durwen spoke with you about these things. Or must you return soon for the midday meal?"

"No, we brought lunch with us." Miggle answered eagerly.

Stevie clapped a hand over his mouth. "Oh, golly," he moaned. "It must have sunk to the bottom of the Bane by now. I was carrying it, and I set it down beside me."

Káolin bowed, laughing. "Then if your lunch rests in Banebottom, you must find another. Will you come into the mountain?"

They looked at each other. Miggle's eyes shone. Arthur nodded slowly.

"Sure we will," Stevie said, as calmly as if the offer had been to go next door for a hamburger. "I'm hungry."

Chapter Ten

Miggle stared around the company in the shadowy room in awe, and Stevie stared equally hard, struggling to keep his curiosity in bounds. There were so many things he wanted to peer at closely or to touch: intricate carvings on chairs and cupboards, wall hangings with the sheen of Miggle's belt, and finely chased designs on the flagons and bowls on the long trestle table.

The table had been lengthened and chairs set around it for the large company. Among those who ate there, laughing and urging bowls and platters of this and that upon them, only the faces of Durwen, Maelin, Rhelemon, and Káolin were known to Arthur. Names flew back and forth, among them Periel, Iolin and Eirin, Arel, Kían and Meruel, Alianor, Illurin and Gilduin; but though introductions had been made, the fair faces were all so sweet and remote that the children could not easily recall which was which. Garym and Túdual they remembered, for their lordly heads were silver-haired, and like the fair and ancient Rhelemon, their skin seemed almost transparent. These elders drank from time to time from tall goblets but spoke little and ate only a few crumbs of the sweet oaten cakes. The children, despite the many distractions, did the meal more than justice, provoking much laughter at their appetites.

"It is many a round of years since we have sat down to table with the children of men." They laughed. "We had forgot what formidable stomachs they have."

"Yes, we have grown far apart," said Durwen soberly. "Not since we first came here from over the sea have the children of men crossed our threshold. Let us hope that we do right now in trusting to the old verses of the dog and the child. We have kept apart because, when long years ago in the old country across the sea we strove to live in peace with men, they feared us and did not long suffer us to move among them. They drove us away from the villages and sweet streams."

He laughed shortly. "Had we the power they so feared in us, we should not have gone so tamely. But those of us who had chosen to stay in that sweet green land for the long love we bore it had made a choice which left us no such strength. In the long age after our elder kin sailed west to the Fortunate Isles, we dwindled, cut off more and more from men until we were at length driven into the fastnesses of the mountain forests. We there were called the Children of Coed y Dugoed Mawr. In your speech that would be the Children of the Wood of the Great Dark Wood."

The children had been bewildered by Durwen's musings. Fortunate Isles? Fastnesses? But one word and its echo rang a familiar note to Miggle's ear.

"Where was this?" She leaned forward, fascinated.

"Coed . . . Coed y Dugoed Mawr? Was it in Wales? Our great-grandmother came from Wales, from a place called Betws y Coed."

"Yes." Maelin answered softly, with an air of surprise. "I remember a fair small village of that name from the days before we were driven to the Great Wood. My sisters and I bought spices and leeks there on many a market day. The women wore tall black hats and trimmed their red flannel petticoats with edgings of taffeta. They feared us, crossing their fingers when they saw our green dresses and blue cloaks come winding down the hills." She sighed. "What was worth one silver penny cost us seven there, and in the end they would not sell to us at all."

"Not our great-grandmother," Miggle protested. "She wouldn't have been like that. I remember her. She was small and plump and had twinkling blue eyes. She used to tell us stories about the Fair Folk . . ." Miggle frowned thoughtfully.

Maelin smiled. "Yes, *y Tylwyth Teg*, the Fair Folk. So they called us, fearing to give us another name. But all this was three hundred years and more before your great-grandmother was a girl."

Arthur blinked and began to look miserable, his doubts returning. Durwen saw, and beckoning to one of the company to bring a cup of *caeren*, a bright clear wine boiled down and sweetened with honey, he tried to put Arthur at ease.

"This will sweeten your mind so that it can listen to your heart," he said shrewdly. "I think I see what ails you. You cannot see where such tales will lead, and so you would choose not to hear them. Perhaps in your heart of hearts you fear that if you believe us and join with us in what you call 'adventure,' you will awake to find only the ashes of a dream and your heart forever lost. At that your courage fails you, and you wish for once to know the ending so that you may choose by reason whether you are with us or no. But reason is not yet wisdom. I think your cousins are in this thing the wiser."

He nodded toward Miggle, who still listened to Maelin. "A keen ear and an eager heart that holds nothing impossible sees much," he said. "Margaret, I see, has an ear for words and for old tales and can leap where reason might never carry her."

Arthur grinned ruefully. His own arguments had been turned back upon him very neatly. "Yes, I guess so. And when she tries it the other way, planning things out all finicky and everything just perfect and tidy, it all ends up in a muddle. I guess Stevie's the only one of us who doesn't try to complicate things into knots. If *he'd* found the old treasure Miggle's been grouching about, he never would have gone and lost it or made up a silly story about it that led nowhere." He flushed. "I might have done just what Miggle did."

"I wonder. But what is this treasure you speak of? Káolin has told me of your search through the Wood. He saw Margaret hiding small objects in the Wood and thought little of it until he watched your search and saw her pretense." Durwen turned to Miggle. "Tell me of this marvelous box and its treasure."

Miggle told her tale again and was encouraged by the growing interest around the table. She ended by saying, with a puzzled frown, "I *still* think it was something valuable or important. It . . . it *felt* that way."

Rhelemon spoke for the first time. Her voice was soft and low. "The child is right, I warrant. Káolin told me of the symbol she scratched somewhere upon a rock, and I have since seen something very like it. Garym and Túdual and I were searching among the ancient books in the Window Hall in another vain attempt to puzzle out the secrets locked in their letters, and we saw this sign many times. But the writing is like none of the tongues of the ancient peoples of our long youth, and so the past of Nũtayẽ must remain in shadow."

"The box was tumbled into the Bane then?" Durwen was thoughtful. "We shall be watchful for news of it. It may be of some importance."

"Excuse me," said Stevie. "But what is 'Nũtayẽ'?"

"This is Nũtayẽ," said Durwen. He indicated the room about them. "That at least was the name the Avenáki, the Indians, gave it. In their tongue the word meant simply 'city,' and we have kept the name, for it was in truth a city once. In a moment we will see more of it if you choose. We sit now only in the least of its halls, on the threshold of the city. We have masked it with the ruin of a house, but once great portals opened here upon the Wood."

Káolin smiled and added in explanation, "The ruin is a precaution we have seldom needed. Few are the hunters who have strayed beyond the round meadow at the head of the greenway. If they do wander close, they are easily led back upon their own trails by a bird call or the snort of a deer. We make such noises quite well! And if any do chance nearer, we still have some skill left in spinning deceptions to the eye." Káolin had abandoned his ill-fitting farm clothes for a blue tunic of some light cloth and looked much less strange in it.

The company at length rose from the table, Rhelemon and Túdual and Garym to walk in the Wood, some to clear the remnants of the meal away, and others to go about their various businesses. Durwen and Maelin led the way to the shadowed end of the room and drew back a woven hanging to reveal the high doors of stone behind. They opened at a touch.

Stevie was not with Arthur and Miggle, and when they turned to look for him, they saw him at the small table by the far window. He turned the carven ivory counters over in his hand and looked up, smiling. "What kind of game is this? The pieces—they're strange." He ran a finger over the fine tracery.

"It is a game we often play," answered Káolin. "It is called *fidchell.*"

"They're beautiful. Will you teach it to me sometime? It looks like it would be fun."

"Indeed he will," said Durwen, bowing. Turning to Arthur, he smiled. "You were right about your young cousin. Strangeness is no bar to him. His heart is whole and his tongue is straight. Grant his curiosity will ever be great enough to keep him so!"

It was a reproof, and even though gently made and fairly, it left Arthur feeling defensive and uncomfortable. He followed Durwen through the doors, Eirin and Kían close behind, and Káolin coming after with Stevie.

A wide passageway sloping gently downward led them to the head of a flight of broad stone steps, which curved from near the roof of a large cavern to its floor some fifty feet below. Down the length of the stair and around the walls of the great chamber that opened out before them, pitch-pine knots in shallow lamps flamed like stars. The children groped down the steps, staring wonder-struck until Maelin gently warned them to watch their feet, for the steps were high and the treads narrow, as if cut for smaller feet than theirs.

The chamber was a great circular hall from which six passages could be seen to radiate, some dark, some lit with lamps. The walls and roof of the chamber itself were covered with lacy stone embroideries of pink and green. The floor was smooth, flagged with a polished black slate so artfully joined that it seemed one single piece. Stone benches sat against the walls and wooden chairs like those in the homely outer room above were gathered around a low round platform of stone where a small fire crackled. In the center of the room stood a fluted column, glittering black and studded with white crystalline flowers.

"It is a natural cave," Durwen explained. "This is beyond the work of hands, though some folk in the dark past of Nũtayẽ have cut the stair and leveled the floor, paving it with skill. The city is so large that even at its height there were caverns left unlit and unexplored. We have sealed off the entrances to the north and many of the northern galleries and passages, since we are not so many and prefer to live in closer comfort."

He stepped to the great column in the room's center and, striking it with a silver rod that hung there for the purpose, rang a silver note that sang in the clear, cool air and echoed down the passages. From the lamplit western passage came five or six of his folk, among them Periel and Meruel.

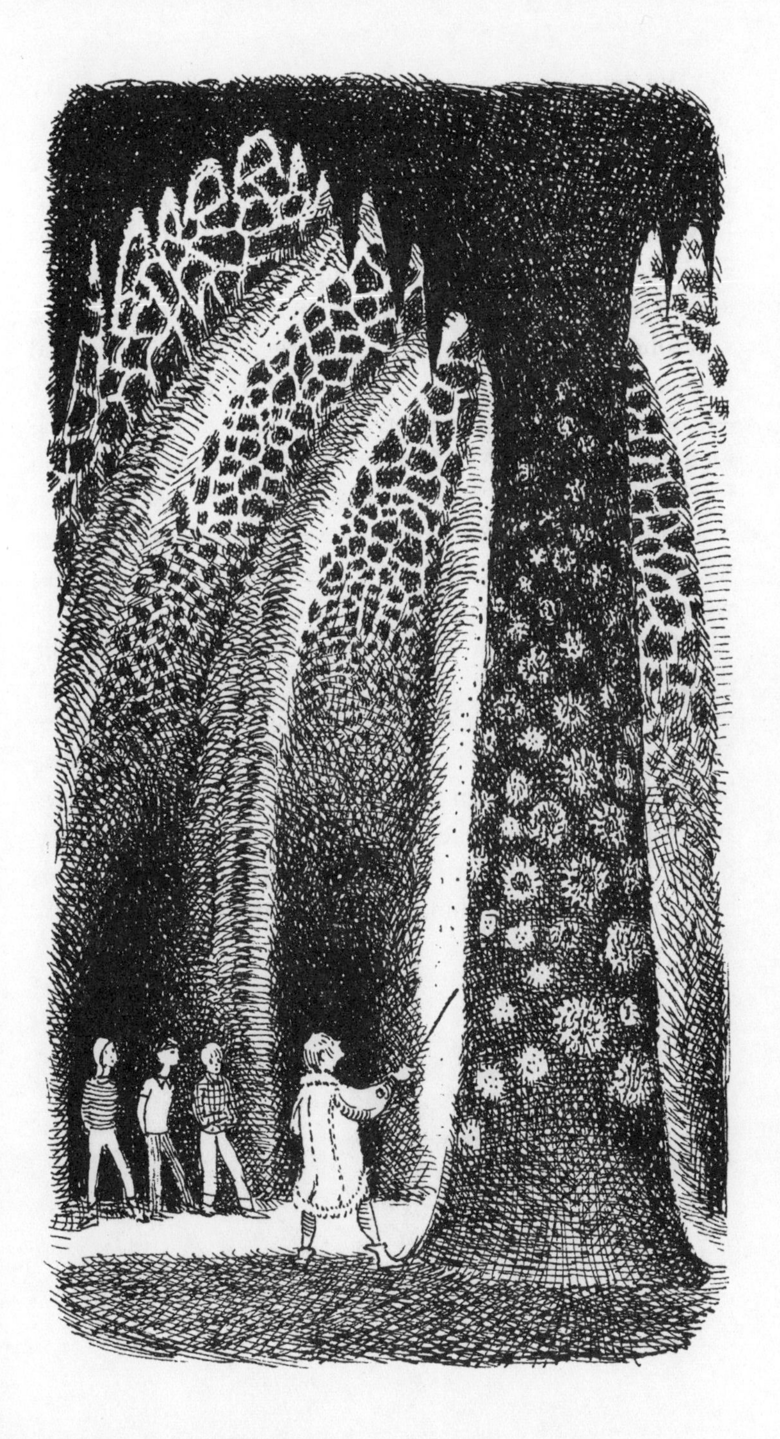

"We will take our friends south to the lowest gallery where they will learn something, I think, of their Bane. Some few of you take tapers and go ahead to light the lamps," he directed. "Periel shall find us three pair of boots, for the lowest levels are often wet and sometimes ankle-deep with mud the river brings."

River? The children looked at each other. What river?

Káolin at the same time eyed the cousins' feet and laughed. "Best bring the largest ones—Kían's or Garan's—if indeed even they will fit. No wonder men leave such loud trails in the Wood when men-children grow such feet!"

Miggle stared at her tennis shoes. She had not thought her feet particularly large, but Meruel's, beside her own, were slim and tiny in their soft embroidered slippers.

"On your return from below you shall have a pair like these to match your belt." Meruel smiled, reading her thought. "Pay Káolin no mind. His laughter blooms easily. He is tempted down among the farms too much because he loves to tease, leaving cave pearls for the eggs he takes and milking cows in the pastures to send them home dry with a silver coin hung between their ears. Yet sometimes his rashness is a happy thing. It has brought you here."

Chapter Eleven

Durwen led them to the chairs by the raised round hearth.

"As we go, I will tell you something of our plight so that you will understand the heaviness this Bane has laid upon our minds and hearts. You have heard that we have been called the Children of Coed y Dugoed Mawr and other names. Some have touched wood and named us the Ellyll, meaning elves or fiends—they knew not which." He looked from one to the other of them. "You may name us as your great-grandmother did, if you wish. It matters little."

He sat in a high-backed chair and watched the small fire thoughtfully. "It matters little. We ourselves have lived beyond the memory of our elders and forgotten the songs that were sung of their deeds in days before the circle of the cold moon was set and the sun grew old. Rhelemon and Túdual and Garym are the only ones left among us who were young in the days of their departing; but they are fading and their lore fails. We had not thought our memory should fade, and so we had few books. When we determined at last to leave Coed y Dugoed Mawr, we thought to make for the passage beyond the Northern Lights to the last home of our folk, or for some one of the Fortunate Isles—for the islands of Aballach, of Tácon or Llanor, or of Ibresíl—though we knew not where they lay, save that the way passed north and to the west."

"We came to the hill above Nant y Ffrith," he said, his eyes distant with remembering a long-ago night. One thousand ahorse and two thousand afoot we were, our treasures bright upon our breasts and brows and our ancient banners blue and silver in the moonlight, broidered with words of power in a tongue strange to all but the eldest among us. We gathered atop Pen-llan-y-gŵr three thousand strong, garbed in green and blue and silver; and we passed over the Alun and over the pass through the Forest of Clwyd like the rushing of a wind. Some saw us pass. The men in Nant y Ffrith barred their doors and trembled behind their shutters. The grass on Mynyth Llanelian and Cefn Du whispered with our passing, and the ferry at Tal-y-cafn plied back and forth until the third hour of morning, when we came at last to Caerhûn."

Durwen's audience waited in suspense as he paused and then continued.

"At Caerhûn the remnants of our kin from Llyn Idwal, from Llyn Dulyn, Melynllyn, and from the fastnesses of Eryri had drawn their boats up on the banks of the river Conwy. In the hour before dawn fifty great coracles slipped through the river mist past sleeping farmhouses and out under the walls and high towers of Conwy to the bay. We sent the ponies onto the slopes above Caerhûn," he recalled, "though they did not leave us willingly."

"What happened to the rest if there were so many?" asked Arthur, pulling on the soft high boots Periel had brought. "There aren't more than twenty or so of you here that I've seen."

"We are forty-one. The others may have passed the barrier of mist and come beyond the moon to the garth of Tir na'nOg, but we were separated from them in a thick fog not far out at sea. All would have been well, but in the fog we heard the crack of heavy sails and the voices of men; and so we raised our oars to keep silence while they passed."

Durwen rose as he spoke and led them to the nearest of the passages. "We never found the others. Then some mornings after, our watch awoke us to a shower of gold that drifted softly from the west. We sang at the sight, thinking it some sign that we had come aright, for it was pollen from—we thought—the apple forests of Aballach.

"And so we came to land. But it was this land. And there were no apple forests, only a Wood beyond belief, long leagues of towering pines that marched from the sea to this last ridge and down onto the foothills beyond. It was this forest that had sent the golden shower of pollen out to sea."

"But—but why did you come *here?* Instead of trying again for your islands, I mean," asked Miggle.

"Well may you ask," Maelin answered. "But the Avenáki—the Indians as you would call them—welcomed us with joy, and we delayed a while. No sooner had we gained some little understanding of their language than they spoke of others like us; always when they spoke gesturing to the west and repeating, 'Nũtayẽ! Nũtayẽ!' until to please them and our own curiosity we came: upriver to the feet of the first mountains and, from there, along the Avenáki trails."

Durwen smiled to see Stevie craning to peer down the

dark passageways that branched off at right angles from the one they walked in.

"Not all curiosity leads to delight, I fear," he said. "We began once more to persuade ourselves that we had reached one of the blessed islands–Llanor, perhaps, or Ibresíl–but we found Nũtayẽ empty and an endless land beyond." He sighed. "Perhaps the islands are no more. Perhaps they, too, have sunk beneath the sea."

He was silent, withdrawn into his own thoughts. Káolin gestured upward, and the children saw that the ceiling was hung with icicles of stone, their tips encrusted with white crystals that caught the lamplight and sparkled down the passage ahead like a river of stars.

"I can never remember whether it's stalactites or stalagmites that come down from the roof," said Miggle, at a loss for anything more appropriate to say.

"Stalactites," Arthur answered. "Just think of T for 'top.' "

"I never thought they would be so beautiful," she said.

Neither had the boys. Growing crystals in fishbowls in science class had given them no idea of what such an underground world would be like, where rock flowed like water and crystals flowered like the crocuses of spring.

"These passages to the left," Káolin explained, "lead to many smaller chambers, some of which we have put to use as storerooms; and off to the right are the great kitchens of the city, which we use but seldom."

The path began to wind downwards and soon came by a short flight of stairs to a wider place, brightly lit, where the footway curved around a gaping hole some two yards across.

"Look down," invited Maelin. "But keep fast hold of us or of the rings set into the wall. It was here that we lost Isura on our first day in Nũtayẽ. Since then we keep it well lit."

Two hundred feet or more below, flickering lights moved over a floor that, like a polished black crystal, reflected the lights as in a mirror. The children craned their necks but could see no end to the shimmering floor.

"That is the Great Hall of Nũtayẽ. We shall look into it on our way, for it is indeed a marvel," Maelin continued. "Yet Nũtayẽ has smaller marvels that please us equally."

She motioned for the children to follow and, with Durwen, led on down the passage that had now begun to wander, passing green pools rimmed with transparent crystals, where white lotos and lilies grew in stone among yellow lily pads of stone. Arthur shook his head. He, and Miggle and Stevie as well, had, in learning about crystals, read how such things grew inside the earth and how oddly water could shape stone; but seeing was another thing. The fact was more beautiful than imagination could have made it. Along the walls thin curtains of stone hung —at times in folds so delicate that Stevie had to touch them to believe that they were not of some heavy silk. Wherever possible, lamps had been placed behind these draperies so that they glowed with the colors of pink and yellow roses.

At last they came into another chamber: domed and large, though not so great as the Hall of the Column above. The floor was strewn with sweet dried grasses, and the walls were smooth, hung in many places with folds of the same stone draperies in white and yellow. Opening off from the main room was a series of small grottoes decked with hanging lamps and crystalline flowers, where low stone couches swelled out from the walls and curious niches were piled with books. In one there were small looms set up, strung with webs of blue and green. In another several of the Fair Folk stitched at garments with flying fingers, while in a third Kían was mending a stringed instrument fashioned somewhat like a lute. In yet another cups and ewers stood by a jade-green pond where the water was deep but as clear as bright glass.

"Come, I shall show you where we are."

Durwen moved to the farthest grotto on the left. It was bare of furnishings, but even so there was room only for himself and the children. Drawing a heavy woven curtain across the archway behind them, he moved to the inner wall and touched a small knob there. A portion of the wall divided into two leaves that swung inward: the shutters to a window that looked down upon the treetops of the Wood and out across the valley to High Egg Ridge. A large tree root grew beside the window, and a fringe of wild strawberry creepers hid it from curious eyes.

"See yonder, far downhill to the south. To the right. There is your Bane and ours. Your house lies not far below it."

"Yes . . . I think I see our old pine tree," said Miggle.

"We will be abreast of the Bane though still some hundreds of feet above it when we reach our lowest level," he explained.

"Golly, the whole mountain must be hollow," Stevie breathed. "How come it doesn't fall in?"

Durwen smiled. "It is strong in the way in which a honeycomb is strong. And, too, the galleries do not extend under the lower slopes but only down through the heart of the mountain."

He closed the window, and they rejoined the others in the outer chamber.

"I can see why you stayed once you got here," Arthur said. He had for the moment forgotten all his doubts. "I wouldn't mind staying here forever."

Miggle nodded in agreement, and Durwen regarded them with some amusement. "Would you?" he asked.

"Never to walk freely in the green meadows and to sing among the apple trees in bloom?" Maelin regarded them with a depth of sadness in her eyes. "Never to see your kin again or to sleep beneath the stars?"

"Not me." Stevie shivered. "That's why I don't understand. Why *didn't* you turn around and go back?"

There was no answer for a long while. Following Durwen, the children entered another passage where steps led downward in a long curve. At a forking of the way it circled to the left, while at its side another stairway, narrow and unlit, kept straight on down.

After some distance Durwen replied. "There were many reasons. It was some time before we found that this was a wide land and no island. We were misled, too, by traces of our elders we had found here: a few inscriptions on the columns and upon the high seat in the Great Hall, graven in our ancient tongue. That is a riddle we have not yet unraveled. There were books as well, most of them in strange characters but some few in a script like to our own. The script was much the same, but the language was strange. Many years Túdual and Garym labored over the books until discouragement came at last. Yet even still we lingered, for this hill was beautiful indeed in those days. Then it was too late for us. We were cut off from the sea by the settlers who came in ships. They cleared the sheltering forest from the valleys and drove the Avenáki westward before them. Hunting and trapping, they ranged the ridges we had come across, and the eastern streams were closed to us by the many settlements of men."

"Perhaps," said Maelin, "perhaps it may have been that if our ancient kind were ever here, as it would seem from these traces and from the tales the Avenáki tried to tell us, why then . . . perhaps they heard it rumored on the wind that men from the east were seeking out these shores in ships. And so they sailed for the Fortunate Isles or Tir na'nOg before it was too late."

"If only the sea were not so far," she sang softly. "If only the mountains not so high, nor the cities of men so many." The notes rang down the stair like a soft ring of bells.

Durwen's face was grim and set.

"We are here for good and all," he said, "and there's an end of it. But this Bane has turned our refuge into a trap, and it is but a matter of weeks or days before the jaws of the trap are sprung. Others than ourselves are periled, too, yourselves and your neighbors not the least."

He did not explain his dark words but led on down the stair.

Chapter Twelve

The curving steps ended, and a gently downward-sloping path went on some fifty yards. The passage widened. On the right they passed an arch where a lamplit flight of steps led down to lower levels yet. Maelin explained that they would return this way after a brief visit to the Great Hall at the end of the curving path. Ahead—they were actually facing north again—a wide arch opened into the Great Hall.

From between the columns that drew up beside the arch, the children could see the Great Hall clearly, but they did not venture far in. The floor was one wide mirror, like a lake of dark water where stars were echoed in the depths. The darkness came not from the crystal floor itself but from its reflection of the deep shadow of the high dome. No lamps could light that shadow, it was so far above.

Around the far borders of the Great Hall, rank upon rank of slim columns gathered close, a dim forest whose boles shone dimly green in the light of the lamps. At the far end larger, more mighty trunks reached upward and outward to each other, the two largest spreading their heavy branches wide. They met above a waterfall, which sprang from the wall and vanished beneath their stony roots. It was this underground river—not wide, but swift—that accounted for the water-shimmer of the lamps' reflections in the crystal floor. It plunged beneath that clear stone, spreading wide underneath the floor and flowing south to narrow again some few yards from where Durwen and Maelin and Káolin stood with the children. There it vanished completely, gathering into a narrow channel and pouring downwards to some lower level. All this could be dimly seen through the floor itself.

The high seat of which Durwen had spoken stood before that far wood and curtain of falling water, on a round-stepped dais some two or three feet high.

"The writing of which I spoke is graven around the topmost step," Durwen said. "We need not pause now to show it, though at some later time you may find it well worth the looking. There are many words in curious tongues and symbols on the steps below, and the chair itself is marvelously wrought."

The company then retraced their steps, returning through the passage to the forking of the ways, where the lamplit stair climbed downwards. A faint trembling beneath their feet told that the river flowed below through a channel or some fissure in the rock. Its destination was the same as theirs—the long galleries below—and near where the stairway ended, it issued forth to flow between low banks through the series of dark chambers ahead.

"There is a narrow stair that slopes downward from the Window Hall to the place where we go now," said Durwen. "But it is in ill repair, and the river is more swift a road."

Five or six of the Fair Folk waited for them at the water's edge. Two were kindling pine-knot flares, which had been fastened to flat discs of wood. Another held by a tether an odd round shell of a boat that Durwen promptly entered. The others, except for the three who had in charge the lamps and the boat, followed. Miggle did so most reluctantly, for every time she reached her foot out, the gap of dark water between the bank and the low-riding boat grew larger. Not until a second rope had secured it, steadying it fast against the bank, did she succeed in climbing in.

At once those left upon the shore set the wooden lamps afloat and freed the boat. Slowly, the wide and shallow scallop moved out into the swifter center of the stream, and there, set amid a flotilla of lights, it moved down the caverns.

"We seldom come below the level of the Great Hall," Durwen said, speaking over his shoulder. "These chambers have no passage but by water. They are cheerless and seem to have been roughly used, perhaps as storerooms. There are broken pinnacles and heaps of shattered flowers here, where higher such lack of care was never shown."

Maelin nodded. "There is an unhappy feeling here. At least it seems so to me. Though the water be sweet and the air clear, here—even as below—I sense the weight of the mountain pressing upon my heart."

"This was so even before the coming of the Bane," said Káolin. "The heaviness the Bane has laid upon the Wood is akin to the heaviness which has oppressed these halls since first we saw them."

"Aye," said Durwen grimly. "And if our fears be true, the two are truly kin." He spoke as if reluctantly. "There seems some evil at the deep root of this ridge, and I fear the Bane has given it the chance of entrance to the outer world. A greater shadow hovers over the hill than the fouling of streams and felling of trees. We have since early spring missed the companionship of animals. The deer fled first and then the gray squirrels. The birds are beginning now to move away westward. Animal folk feel keenly any disturbances in their world."

"But not all are moved to flee," Káolin said. "Lizards scuttle over the Bane. Those animals who live on death are increasing, ravening. Crows, weasels, wildcats–we see more of these every day–yet we know not what food they find. Some few chickens, perhaps, and ground hog kits from across the low meadows, fat and unsuspecting. Yet that cannot be enough."

"We haven't lost any chickens. Not yet, anyhow," said Miggle. "But there have been an awful lot of crows, come to think of it."

"If you're right about there not being anything for them to eat," Arthur asked, "why do they stay? Or do they eat each other?"

"No." Káolin's face showed his puzzlement. "They range these hills, growing lean and wild-eyed, never straying far from the Bane. It is as if they were drawn and held here."

"What I can't see is how the digging machine men can stand it," Stevie said. "Besides its being creepy, it must be awfully dull, digging away all day in an ugly hole."

"Because it's a job, that's why," Arthur said. "Uncle

Owen says at least it gives jobs to lots of people over in Tipple and around who need them."

"The truckers, maybe," Miggle said. "But the others —the ones who work in the Bane itself—aren't from around here. They all live together at the tourist home next to the Post Office in High Egg. The postmistress told Mother they keep to themselves. 'Uppish,' she said. And they all go away every weekend as soon as work is over."

Durwen signed for those in front in the boat to use their wide paddles to slow it. The farthest of the floating lamps had come to a halt thirty or forty yards ahead.

"Men, too, are drawn here," he said, turning again. "Káolin and I myself have seen armed guards: ill-favored men and unfriendly, such as the one you yourselves have seen. There are others who drift in and stand about in twos and threes to watch the work. It would be well if you spoke of this at home so that they will know to take care to lock up well at night. But here we are! Take care, take care!"

The roar of falling water sounded ahead. Durwen cautioned the two of his people in the front—Eirin and Illurin—as they worked to slow the boat to a stop despite the current, which would have swept it hard against the low stone bridge directly ahead. It was this bridge—so low that nothing but the water could pass under it—that had stopped and held the floating lights.

Once on the shore, the cousins could see why the bridge had been set so low upon the stream. The water flowed under it and poured in a great swirling rush through a wide hole that spanned the smooth stream bed.

"It falls from here to the water level far below—the level at which Banebottom and your own spring stand," Durwen explained. "It falls with great force, and whatever dwells in those depths cannot force its way up the narrow passage against such a crushing weight. But it well may be that it has broken into the flooded lower galleries of one of the old shaft mines. The shafts were sunk deep, and some sent their searching fingers deeper than was wise. But the upper shafts were filled with rubble and securely capped, and so the evil found no escape until the Bane delved deep to meet it. Or such is our fear. It would interest me to know what your neighbor knows of this. We know that he was sorely frighted one day as he worked his small mine but could find out nothing of it."

"Mr. Dekany?" Miggle asked. "Golly, he never said anything. But I'll find out if you want."

The little company joined their strength to draw the boat out of the water so that the current would not batter it against the rock shore or the bridge. The roof was low and the floor uneven, making it awkward work despite the lightness of the craft, which was cunningly made from wickerwork covered with skins and sealed with pitch. It was set down at last near a second hole, the size of that into which the river poured, in a wide channel scooped into the floor.

"Did the stream use to run here?" asked Arthur. "It looks like it might have run along here and turned down that passage." He pointed to a black opening in the dark shadows off to the right, along the western wall.

"It seems likely," Durwen answered, "though it must have been in the deeps of time before the water carved its present downward path. Also, the lower room where we go now must once have known the river's rush," he said. "Come, follow me."

Torches were lit from the lamps by the barrier bridge, and in their brighter flare the children saw that the hole was a shaft, leading straight downwards. Stout rungs had been set at close intervals down its wall, and now Eirin and another nimbly made their way down this ladder, bearing torches to light the room below. Durwen and Maelin went next and waited at the bottom as the children followed, slowly and less surely. Káolin came after, and Illurin remained above.

The chamber was low-roofed and damp, and the rough floor was pocked with puddles of mud and water. In the eastern wall a low passage sloped downward. In the center of the floor was what Durwen had brought them to see.

It was a great round inset of stone—"like a monster manhole cover," as Stevie later described it. It fit so tightly into the floor that the seam was almost invisible, and it was sealed tightly. Yet, seal or no, heavy dankness and a piercing unease filled the room, far stronger and more dismaying than it had been in the river chambers above. Miggle shivered as she watched over the boys' shoulders while they traced out the puzzling letters encircling the stone.

"Those words set about the outer edge are in our ancient speech," Maelin explained. "It says, as nearly as I can put it in your tongue:

> "Despair be his who breaks these seals,
> Slavery his who unbinds the bonds;
> For then teeth shall rend the hills
> And a shadow cover the lands.

"We would seal this room solid, but it would be to no avail so long as the Bane lies below to spread its greed and dust and dark water. This Minshew, whom we think has rashly and unknowingly unbound those bonds, is enslaved at least by greed and may be in danger of a more bitter servitude. Perhaps his greed drew the evil, as he in turn may have been drawn by it."

She smiled sadly. "I remember him as a young man farther north upon these hills. He came with a small truck and a huge saw, which he set up under a roughly built shed in a fair dell. His hand was light, and he began by cutting only trees which had known disease or wounds, and thinning where trees grew too thickly. But he changed. He ended in felling all but those too slender yet to be of use. Those who now harvest among the trees hereabouts take care to choose from here and there and to replant as they go, but he left only a decaying heap of sawdust and a ragged hillside of stumps and tangles of lopped branches. These lumbermen today are shepherds of the Wood, but he was the wolf who ravaged on the slopes."

"But you don't know what this—this evil is?" asked Arthur. "You all keep saying 'perhaps' and 'maybe.' "

"That is all we say because we only suppose. Have I not made this clear?" Durwen frowned. "We *know* nothing beyond what is written here at our feet. The old books keep their silence. The inscriptions in the Great Hall are of no help. They are for the most part fragments of song from our long past and of the green days before the reshaping of the lands and seas. They speak of no dark things."

Maelin tried to explain. "It is our hearts which tell us

most surely that what dwells below is some power which hates us, which hates things that live and flourish freely. Put the ugliness and destruction of the Bane itself from your minds for a moment. Do you not feel that here in this chamber something more than man's greed troubles this mountain?"

Miggle answered slowly, puzzling. "Yes, it *is* almost as if you could feel somebody hating you through the walls. But how are we supposed to be able to help? You've explained and shown us everything and watched us as if you expected us to *do* something like . . . like say a magic word that sets everything right."

The Fair Folk laughed ruefully.

"I suppose that *is* what we have hoped for." Maelin smiled. "The old verse says naught but:

" 'Brindle dog and darkling child
Shall find the way within the wild.
Stone and feather fast en-isled!
Silver-eyed the dog alone
Can find the way beyond the throne
To the feather and the stone.'

"There is more, each verse less clear than its fellow before. It is truly a riddle. Yet tradition tells and the weight of the words in our own tongue suggest that it has some deeper import than we can put a name to. So you see, we are as helpless as you to know the ending of the tale we walk in. The end of the song speaks of freeing the folk, and we can only hope that this means freedom from this thing we fear. We fear a fate that would see your fair valley decayed, the animals fled, the green things choked with dust, and little left but the brown earth and thirsting villages.

Such may well be the shadow meant in this writing at our feet: a disease that once rooted in man's heart would blind him to the beauty he stripped from the earth and felled with his forests. Such a rift between man and the rest of life would not soon be mended."

"Come, my lady," Durwen said. "Now you look as if you would indeed ask if the children have a magic word to heal the breach the Bane has made. Come, let us up and out of this heavy-hearted place." Taking her by the hand, he moved to the ladder and the lighter world above.

Stevie and Eirin were the last to leave the huddled cavern. As they waited their turn at the ladder, Stevie pointed to the low passage opening off the eastern wall.

"Where does that go?" he asked. "Durwen said the river must have gone through here. Where did it come out? Can you still get out that way, or is it too steep?"

Eirin laughed, putting his hands to his ears. "You will wash me down it with a flood of questions! To begin with, it once opened out under a broad shelf of stone some hundred yards above what is now the Bane. Some of the water was diverted into nearby springs, and so the river was much less full than above—not truly a river. The passage is quite steep and grows more narrow and low as it proceeds, but Kían and I explored its length soon after we first came to Nũtayẽ. We sealed it then against intruders." He smiled. "We very nearly sealed ourselves at the bottom—we loosed such a great fall of rocks. Now, why do you ask?"

Stevie followed in his turn up the ladder rungs.

"Oh, just wanted to know," he answered, and the words echoed hollowly down the round shaft. "What about the one up here?"

"The one what up here?" asked Káolin, giving him a hand up into the channel in the stone floor above.

"The passage. There where the old river went when it ran along up here." He nodded toward the carven channel that curved westward from where they stood.

"I have never gone that way, though some–Kían, I think, and Enniaun–have done so. There is a long drop from this level to that on which the river made its escape from under the hills. It fell in a steep series of falls through jewel-like caverns and then slid swiftly out to join a stream that still flows north at the feet of the hills."

"Where is that?" Arthur had joined them to help with lifting the boat once more around the foaming spillway where the river disappeared and past the wide flat bridge.

"It is a tree-lined stream, not deep, which moves through meadows and past high stone barns. I have been down that way through the Wood when 'trading' for oats." He smiled.

"I know where that is!" Miggle said. She and Maelin held the torches to light the way front and back. "That's over the Ridge. It runs through Colwyn a ways. It's called Lickpiddy Creek. You remember, Arthur–once when we were at Great-Aunt Margaret's, we went wading in the creek there?"

"It is a pleasant place," said Káolin. "But the opening was long ago sealed off like the others because we did not care to guard it, and the access is reported difficult, down many long flights of steps. Nũtayẽ in its time was a city of many gates; therefore, a rich and peaceful city, it would seem. Our one gate takes all our skill to hide and defend."

The trip upriver was slow. All but Maelin and Miggle, the torch-bearers, put hand to paddle and plied stoutly against the current. When at last the company had climbed to the highest level and the homely room that was the threshold of Nũtayẽ, the children were warm and tired.

While they pulled off the borrowed boots and then gratefully accepted an offer of cups of sweet *caeren*, Maelin tried to cheer their gloom.

"Come, you must not let the darkness shadow your own hearts. To be able to face knowledge of the dark power and still to hold fast to beauty and laughter is truly to walk in freedom, for you as for us. Do not puzzle yourselves what to do. Wait and listen. The answer may drop like a flower petal in its own time.

"We shall be waiting here to learn that the petal has dropped." She smiled. "You are our good omen." With these words she turned to beckon Willy from his sleep on the hearth. Periel handed Miggle her parasol.

Durwen held up a delaying hand as the children moved toward the outer door.

"Be cheerful, but let us hope that in the open air you will not forget what you have heard and seen here inside the mountain. You know less of us than you think and must trust us perhaps against your reason." He paused, as if measuring them. "Old tales once said that there was no truth in us, that we were thieves; and more, that those who crossed our threshold and ate our food were forever imprisoned in our fair dwellings. Some told, with more cause, that those who sat down with us to sup found upon their leaving that the earth had circled the sun so many times since first they entered that their homes and folk had passed away and strangers plowed their fields. Do you think that we have spoken fairly to deceive?" He watched Arthur especially keenly.

"You have said that you would not mind staying here forever. Are you sure that this outer door will open to you? Or if it does–you well may find a desert at your feet, your house decayed, and all you care for gone." He spoke in deep and threatening tones and seemed to grow before their eyes, to loom tall and terrible with red-gold locks as bright as a molten sun and alien silver eyes. He raised his hand as if it held some power he might choose to wield against them. The room was thrown into deep shadow by his radiance.

Arthur trembled, but knew he was being tested and so stubbornly held his ground. He had failed the first test offered him in this room, and this time he was determined to trust these strange folk. That was what they wanted. Miggle and Stevie had fallen back a step in alarm. When Durwen smiled upon them and lowered his hand, they saw that he was still no taller than Arthur. It was as if for the moment past they had been looking through a distorting lens.

Durwen seemed to await an answer.

Miggle spoke first. "It's that you aren't sure of *us*, isn't it? Why? We felt that creepy unliveness down below, so of course we know it's real. The same goes for thinking all of you are–well, O.K. I mean, if we see something and feel it inside, too, well . . . that's as sure as anybody can be, isn't it?"

"Anyhow, why would you want to keep us here?" asked Stevie. He met Durwen's gaze gravely. "It wouldn't make sense. If we're to help getting the Bane stopped, how could we do it from in here?"

Arthur nodded. "We sure can't *tell* anybody about your being here, either, so your secret's safe with us. Uncle

Owen and Aunt Vi would think we'd gone soft in the noodle."

"Besides," said Stevie, "I'm hungry. So let's go. It's still a long time until supper, and I don't want to miss Aunt Vi's teatime." Then, remembering his manners, he blushed and mumbled, "Thanks for lunch and everything."

Everyone laughed. "One who deals in essentials indeed!" exclaimed Durwen, laughing with the others.

"Well," said he, "since we are joined in league against the Bane, I deem it good that we should part in laughter. Come." He motioned them to the door. "If you have word for us, of good or ill, bring it to your Throne Rock at the third hour of the afternoon. Not tomorrow, but the day after. Káolin or some other of us will be there each day from then on to wait the chance of your coming. Now fare you well!"

At the foot of the long shadowy corridor of beeches, Káolin saluted them in farewell, calling after them in ringing tones, "May your tea be sweet and your supper hearty. . . . And take care!"

Chapter Thirteen

The Wood was shadowy and dim. When the children came out into the open at the township dam, they saw that the sun had already dropped behind the Ridge. Afternoon was shading into the long evening.

"That's funny," said Miggle. "How long *were* we inside the hill? Any more than three hours? It didn't seem that long even."

"Four hours, maybe," said Arthur. He frowned at the sky. "We did walk a good long way, and that boat trip back up the river took three or four times as long as the ride down. Still, it couldn't all have taken more than four hours."

Stevie shrugged. "So what if it did? I don't think it was the same in there. It was kind of like the first day of vacation—you know, like the clock had slowed down all of a sudden and there was time to *see* everything you looked at. And that makes time seem just—fuller. No, that doesn't work, does it? That would make time shorter than it felt, wouldn't it?" He left off, confused.

"That's what it was like the last time." Arthur frowned. "But now it seems the other way around."

"Maybe Stevie's right," Miggle said slowly. "But maybe it's that time is—is *deeper* inside, and we only skate along on top of it out here, so it seems to go faster."

"But last time . . ." Arthur began to protest, but walked on, a niggling doubt beginning to furrow his brow. If time could work differently from one time to another. . . . What if Durwen had been playing with them instead of testing them, or him? What if—what if they had been in there for days?

He pushed the thought away but quickened his pace down the trucking road. Miggle and Stevie hurried to keep up. Willy padded after.

"You're not afraid about what Durwen said, are you?" asked Miggle breathlessly.

"Of course not. Don't be silly. He was just trying us out. I knew it was O.K. anyway. After all, I was inside before and ate their stuff—or drank their milk anyhow—and got out. So I knew it wasn't true about never being able to leave."

Miggle grinned mischievously. "But you were only *on* the threshold of Nũtayẽ that first time. You hadn't crossed it. And it was probably our own milk you drank."

Arthur's frown deepened. He did not at all like the thought that time could speed up or slow down like a railway train. It wasn't right. You couldn't explain it. It was all very good spinning words around puzzles like this thing under the mountain, but he preferred to *know* what he knew was true and to think of all the rest as—well, as interesting stories or games but still make-believe. Had he known what it was like to fall head-first into a tale, he would not have talked so much about making games as real as possible. No, it was better when there was a good clear line. Not to know whether you were walking around in Saturday or Tuesday? It would sound exciting in a story, but it would be awful to have it truly happen.

"Oh, galoshes!" said Miggle. "Listen. There's the bell. It must really be late. Sounds like Mother's ringing her wrist off. Come on, you guys."

They ran. Arthur was cheered at the sound of the old handbell. Aunt Vi would not be ringing them in from the hill if they had been gone past Saturday.

Supper was on the table. Time *had* sped while the children were under the mountain, but to Arthur's mind an extra hour or two could easily be explained by their interest in what they were seeing. They were less easily explained to his aunt. Mrs. Arthur had wanted Miggle's help with supper, and though the younger girls had helpfully fed and amused Rover, she had been running up and down the cellar steps between stacking a new batch of bowls in the kiln for firing and cutting up vegetables for the stew.

"So don't anyone say a word if we have bits of pottery in the *sauce au vin Medoc* and carrots in the kiln," she warned as they sat down to supper.

"Glazed carrots?" asked Mr. Arthur innocently, unfolding his napkin.

The children groaned. "Oh, *Daddy!*" said Miggle.

"Just for that," said Mrs. Arthur, dipping the ladle into the stew, "I'll save all the bits of pottery for you."

Toward the end of the meal Mr. Arthur paused in cutting a piece of cheese to go with his apple pie.

"Margaret, I almost forgot. Where was it you said you lost that box?"

Miggle looked up, startled, and answered through a mouthful of pie.

"I' the Wood by the stripping." She swallowed. "Why?"

"And it was carved like a big walnut? About so big?" He measured with his hands.

She nodded.

"Well, I've found it for you." He took a large bite of pie.

"You *have?* Oh, Daddy, where? And where is it?" She pushed back her chair.

"Sit down, Miggle dear. Your father's mouth is full, and *he* wouldn't think of answering you until he's swallowed."

The younger girls giggled. Arthur and Stevie barely kept their curiosity in control. Miggle teetered miserably on her chair.

"There! Sorry, honey. I didn't know it was so important to you or I wouldn't have forgotten to bring it down. It was up on the chicken-coop roof, stuck in the top of one of the ventilator pipes. I put it in the hallway of the coop and then forgot to bring it down with me. How do you suppose it could have gotten up on the . . ."

Miggle was gone, banging through the hall, library, and sun-porch doors into the graying dusk.

"It really is important, kind of," said Stevie to his astonished aunt and uncle. He was saved from having to explain by a cross between a small roar and a large shriek that floated through the open window.

"Daddy! Daddy, come quick!"

It was followed by a frantic barking from Willy.

"I don't like the sound of that." Mr. Arthur knocked his chair over in his hurry.

"Maybe it's those spookery men who hang around the Bane," said Stevie, close upon his heels.

From the sun porch they could hear Miggle shouting at the top of her lungs through the chicken-coop door. She apparently had barricaded herself in the hallway that ran from front to back, between the old hens' room and the pullets' room.

"Weasels! Daddy, it's weasels. They're in with the little hens!"

"I'm coming, honey. Hush up and wait," he called. He ran back indoors to return with a shotgun and a handful of shells, which he thrust into his pocket.

The boys had ventured past the spring to the corner of the chicken-run fence. They were delighted; and if Arthur had not fancied himself too grown up, he would have been jumping up and down in silent glee like Stevie. Willy ran up and down the length of the fence, his hackles high.

"Uncle Owen? They're still in there," Arthur whispered. "Unless they cut out when old Mig started to screech."

"No, they're still inside," his uncle answered calmly. "Listen to those hens flapping and squawking." He loaded both barrels of the shotgun.

"Margaret?"

"Yes, Daddy?" Her voice floated back through the dusk.

"Now I want you to flick on the light switch right there beside the pullets' door and then start banging on the wall. I want to get them out here in the run. All right?" He motioned the boys back beyond the spring.

"All right." There was a pause, and then the lights shone

through the screened windows. A fearful banging boomed through the wooden coop. The chickens, what with the noise and being able to see the enemies in their midst, flapped more wildly and screeched bloody murder, as Stevie aptly put it afterwards.

"I wonder if chickens get heart attacks," he whispered to Arthur.

"Shhh!" Arthur gave him a lofty look of disapproval. Then, as a dark shadow moved against the square of light at the small hatch-door opening from the coop into the run, he forgot his dignity and repeatedly dug his elbow into Stevie's ribs.

"Cut it out! I see, I see!" Stevie hissed.

The shadow dipped its head this way and that, then moved sinuously down the plank that the chickens used as passageway from the stilt-perched coop into the large wire-fenced run. Miggle was still banging. The dark form was followed by a second and a third, and when they had gathered at the bottom of the plank, they were joined by a fourth and fifth, larger even than the first.

The boys shrank further into the shadows. They looked at each other, both remembering Durwen's and Káolin's tale of the growing number of animals of prey. Arthur's high spirits deserted him.

Mr. Arthur's mouth moved in a silent exclamation. Slowly, he shouldered the shotgun, hoping fiercely that his movements, behind a fencepost and beyond the yellow light, were unseen. The weasels caught a scent, probably on the light breeze that moved across the spring pond, and they scattered like streaks of dark quicksilver.

The shotgun roared twice through the dusk. Miggle stopped banging.

Mr. Arthur kicked at the fencepost in disgust.

"Missed! The biggest, nastiest vermin I've ever seen around here, and I missed!"

He turned to the boys. "Did you see that? Five of them! It will be a miracle if we have a whole pullet left." He shrugged. "Ah well, come along. Let us free our damsel, close the hatch, and count our casualties, and then back to the apple pie."

Miggle peered through a knothole in the front coop door, then opened to them thankfully. She clutched the walnut box under one arm and still held a shovel, which she had used for the banging.

"Oh, Daddy! Did you see them? They were awful. Did you get them?"

He gave her a squeeze. "No, I'm afraid not. I could have sworn I had two of them dead center, but they kept right on going. You were great, though! If ever I need the chicken coop knocked down, the job is yours. The poor thing was shaking on its stilts."

Miggle smiled with an effort. Then she poured out what had happened.

"I was in here," she said. "And I heard the chickens rushing around in there, so I opened the top half of the door to look; and those–things, those weasels were under the roost, moving up and down the baseboard on this side. Then they saw me looking, and all rushed at the door. Boy, did I pull it shut quick and fasten it! Then I yelled."

"And very well indeed, I must say." Her father laughed.

"You sounded like a wounded *Amphisbaena*," said Arthur.

"A what?" She stared blankly, and then remembered.

"Oh, Dub, you're awful. And those poor little chickens," she moaned. "I bet they're all crunched to bits."

Mr. Arthur unfastened the door at top and bottom. "Yes, I'm afraid so. Let's have a look."

The room was a chaos. Feathers still fluttered, and at the opening of the door the pullets scattered in new panic. Oddly enough, only three chickens had been killed; and though three or four more had been mauled and shaken, they had lost only dignity and feathers. Under the roosts, in nests, and under scrabbling heaps of other chickens, wild-eyed frowsy birds shrank from the kind, reaching, exploring hands. Stevie shut and fastened the small hatch. Arthur filled a coffee can with cracked corn from a hallway bin, and the sight of food at an unexpected hour effected a marvelous recovery in many of the young hens. Margaret helped her father to smear a sticky red medicine on the bald spots on the necks of two who had apparently been swung about by their neck feathers. Without this foul-tasting protection, the others would soon have been tempted to peck and finish what the weasels had left undone.

Mr. Arthur put the dead chickens into a bucket in the hallway with a warning to the children not to touch them.

"You don't know what else those vermin have had their teeth into. I'll bury these tomorrow." He shook his head. "I can't figure why there wasn't more damage done. And the creatures didn't even eat their chicken dinners, though they must have had plenty of time. Peculiar. Well," he said, "come along. Clean your shoes off on the mat in the hall.

"And wash your hands before you go back to the table," he called as Stevie, having cleaned his shoes off, ran down the path to the house. The others followed more slowly, Miggle keeping close to her father and clutching the box to her breast.

"You O.K.?" Arthur whispered.

She nodded solemnly and shaped with her mouth the silent words, "I'll tell you later."

Once the pie was finished, the opening of the box drew everyone into the library. The work on the box itself was admired as it was passed from hand to hand. Mrs. Arthur alone guessed correctly the way the lock must work, but she passed it on to Miggle for opening.

"Oh." Trish was clearly disappointed at the "treasure" inside. "I thought it would have jewels in it. It isn't even gold, I bet."

Mr. Arthur weighed it in his hand. "No, I hardly think so. But it's a nice piece of work, whatever it is. No careless saw or file marks of the sort you usually find on brass work. You say you lost it? But where did you find it in the first place, Margaret? The box is one of Dekany's. I can see that."

She rubbed a forefinger nervously under her nose and then looked up through her lashes to watch her father's expression while she admitted having been dredging in the spring.

"Dredging inside the spring? With my minnow net?" He was more puzzled than angry. "What on earth ever put such a thing in your head?"

"I don't know." She shrugged uncomfortably. "It just seemed like a good idea. It was kind of silly, I guess. I mean, there *shouldn't* have been anything to find."

Her eyes shone as she looked pointedly at Stevie and

Arthur. "That's another sign it's something important, isn't it? It was almost asking me to find it."

Her mother reached out a hand for the treasure and turned it over thoughtfully.

"You're right, Owen. It is a beautiful piece of work. I can't think where it is I've seen something like this bit on the handle. Never mind. At least you can be sure it's not a piece off of a lamp or furniture or whatnot, Miggle. It's far too finely made for that—unless it was a very very old and rare lamp indeed." She handed it back.

Miggle wrapped it carefully in her handkerchief and shut it up in the box. The rest of the evening—through the dishwashing, the evening comics, and a game of chess with Stevie—she kept it close at hand or in her lap. Stevie won as usual. Miggle, in trying to think ahead, often missed the immediate danger to her queen.

Arthur and his uncle worked on the map and a letter to the Governor.

At nine o'clock the three older children announced that they were tired and thought they would get ready for bed. They promised to be quiet so as not to wake Rover, who had only a while before dropped off to sleep after a third request for a drink of water.

This voluntary withdrawal—just before "Secret File 13" came on the radio—was to Trish and Kit highly suspicious. After a whispered conference they yawned, said a sleepy good night, and hurried upstairs themselves.

Miggle, already in her nightgown and robe, was in the back bedroom whispering with the boys. The box was open, and Stevie was inspecting the gold-colored "key."

"You know, I saw a little star shape like this somewhere up there," he said. "Not in the books, where Rhelemon said. I didn't see any of the books. It was somewhere else—a carving, I think."

Miggle saw the girls in the half-open doorway. She made violent signals toward the floor and the library below and beckoned them in.

Arthur looked uncomfortable. "You're not going to go through the whole thing for them, are you?"

"Why not?"

"Yes, why not, Dub?" said Kit. "Why not what?"

"Chatterboxes. They'd tell your mom and dad. And they'd think we were nuts for sure."

"We would *not*. Tell what?"

"Sometimes, Arthur Arthur, I could hit you." Miggle glared. "Who cares what anybody thinks? Anyhow, the nuttier anybody thinks we are, the safer Nũtayẽ is. And five heads couldn't be worse than three when the three haven't had a single good idea yet."

"There's the letter. It's a good letter," said Arthur.

"Suppose it is? Even if the Governor galloped all the way here on a white charger the minute he read it, it might be too late. Ouch!" She winced. "Don't you pinch me, you—you nurd!"

"Oh, come on, Dub," said Stevie. "They'll pester until we tell, anyway."

"*They'll* think we're making it up," Dub grumbled.

But they did not. Trish even had an idea.

Chapter Fourteen

"If the black pond is all that dangerous," said Trish, "wouldn't filling it in help? I mean, whatever it's reaching out for, then it couldn't get at it. For a while at least?"

The others, seated in a circle on the floor, looked blank.

"Well of course, featherhead. That's the whole point," said Dub.

"Then let's make Mr. Minshew fill it up."

"Us and who else?"

"What are you getting at?" Stevie leaned forward.

"Yes, what?" asked Miggle. She knew that eyebrows-up smug look on her sister's small face.

"Easy. Just tell Daddy how Stevie fell in."

"Heck, no!" said Stevie. "D'you want Mom and Dad to come pack Kit and me up and take us home to Johnstown?"

Miggle waved her hands. "Wait, wait . . . it's true. We *are* dumb. You wouldn't get into trouble; Mr. Minshew would. After all, it wasn't your fault. All sorts of stuff was sliding in. Daddy could sue them for having a—a what d'you call it?—an 'attractive nuisance,' and they'd have to fill it in. Or he might be able to get one of those court order things so they would have to do it right off. Mr. Padgett would know."

Arthur nodded reluctantly. "It sounds worth a try. I'm for anything that'll slow the Bane down for a day or two. That's all it will do, but that's something."

"What do you mean, 'that's all'? Banebottom is the worst place. If it's filled in, the evil won't spread."

"Oh, don't be a goop, Mig. That 'evil beneath the mountain' stuff is just a way of talking; like poetry. There will still be coal and there will still be greedy old Minshew's men to dig it, and the Bane will keep on spreading no matter how many holes they have to fill in. That's the only evil there is."

"That's what *you* say."

Stevie shivered. "You're the one who's goopy, Dub. This afternoon we were clear inside a mountain and feeling something awful down there aching to get out. And here you are talking as if it's only a greedy old man."

Miggle frowned. "Maybe the Fair Folk couldn't absolutely say for sure that it was more. But I'm going to find out if Mr. Dekany knows anything about it all. They seemed to think he might; maybe because of his mine."

Arthur shifted uneasily. "Well, even if there was something down there, what's to stop the stripping from making another hole deep enough to meet up with it?"

"Nothing so far," Miggle agreed. "But if they had to fill everything up again as soon as they got the coal out, it would at least be safer, wouldn't it?"

Everyone nodded in agreement, and Kit was elected to go "spill the beans" about Stevie's mishap at Banebottom. The Arthurs, looking stern and upset, came upstairs to find out exactly what had happened. Miggle, Arthur, and Stevie again told the whole tale of their meeting the armed guard, of the black lake and shifting hills, and of Káolin's timely rescue. By agreement they said nothing of the caves and as little as possible of Káolin's folk.

"And your friend said that one of the bulldozers had fallen into this lake as well?" Mr. Arthur frowned. "It must be quite a pit. We're all very lucky indeed that this Colin was nearby. I should have thought that you and Margaret would have known better than to let Stevie go off by himself, Arthur."

"Yessir."

"Hm, well, no harm done. But I want it understood that none of you are to set foot into the Bane again. Is that clear?"

"Oh dear, not at all?" said Miggle. "But we—we might *have* to." She had not foreseen this objection.

Her father pointed a warning finger. "No 'buts.' This is no fooling matter." He turned to Mrs. Arthur. "I'll phone Rob Padgett tomorrow afternoon as soon as we're back from your Aunt Margaret's. We'll see what Judge Carsten can do to force Minshew into filling these deep pits as he goes instead of waiting until he's through digging. We can give him a good scare by threatening a lawsuit over this. It may slow things down a bit, give us time to round up all the legal ammunition we can find."

She nodded. "Yes. I think, though, dear," she said, "that you ought to make the children give you their promise not to go into the Bane. I see alarm signals being blinked back and forth and doubt that anything short of a sacred oath will keep them out. Somehow I don't think 'spookery' shotgun guards will. And no crossing of fingers," she added shrewdly. "I'll go downstairs to make sure that we're locked up snugly."

The promise was duly but reluctantly sworn, and the children were left to finish getting ready for bed. Stevie had his temperature checked, but it was quite normal, and he hadn't even a sniffle to show for his dunking.

Arthur was secretly relieved at the promise they had been required to give. There was no telling what ideas Miggle and Stevie might get into their impractical heads, he thought; and the little girls would go along with whatever sounded interesting at the moment. It had been a good idea to tell Uncle Owen after all. The lake *was* dangerous, and kids couldn't do much against a big company all bristling with lawyers and armed guards. That was another thing: it was pretty silly of Durwen to talk as if a bunch of kids and a dog could save a whole mountain singlehanded. And it *was* only the Ridge that was in danger. That stuff about it spreading everywhere—that was as queer as the stories about their having come to the mountain over three hundred years ago. Things like that didn't happen. Funny, though. It had all sounded natural enough while they were down in the caverns. But it didn't make sense now that he thought about it. He subdued his pillow with a violent punch in its middle and stretched out on the bed with his hands locked together under the pillow behind his head so that it covered his ears and shut out the groaning of the Elephants.

Stevie turned out the light and crawled into the other side of the bed. He knew that something was bothering old Dub, something he didn't want to talk about. Dub was —he was unhappy. That was it. "Unhappy." It didn't sound right, not for Dub, who had been full of ideas and jokes all the other summers they had been together. Now he was dragging his heels. He was different, sort of "on and off."

"Dub? You awake?" he whispered.

Arthur breathed heavily and did not move, but Stevie knew he was awake.

He wants to desert us! was the thought that came into Stevie's mind. He repeated it to himself, trying to figure it out. He wants to. But he can't make up his mind.

Stevie was still miserably awake three hours later, at midnight, when Willy began making a din up in the barn: barking, whining, and—so it sounded—throwing himself against the barn door. The noise was quite loud and rang insistently against the house and through the screened windows across the back wall of the boys' room. Arthur slept on, though Stevie couldn't understand how. Sticking his fingers in his ears, he counted to a hundred. When he took them out, Willy was howling, which was worse than the barking. It was enough, he thought, to wake everybody from Ridgebottom Farm to Barhatches', but, unaccountably, no one seemed to be stirring. Arthur was stretched out catty-cornered on the bed, his pillow on the floor and one arm hanging over the edge. He lay solid and unstirring, breathing through his open mouth. The day's frown was gone. He looked more than ever like his father. Stevie, who was beginning to be frightened at the note of anger and terror in Willy's howls, put out a hand to jostle his cousin awake, but then drew back. Only babies were afraid of noises in the dark—or that was what Dub would say. He was as grumpy as a grownup when he first awakened.

It was not really dark except in the room itself, away

from the moonlight that spilled over the wide window seat. Carefully, so as not to jiggle the bed, Stevie slid one leg out, then the other, then slowly eased his weight off the mattress. The rag rug was soft under his feet, but the boards beneath creaked alarmingly. He looked quickly at Dub, but there was still no sign of life there.

Once on the window seat with his feet tucked up beneath him, he watched and listened carefully to the night shadows and sounds. Except for Willy, now whining with a high hysterical sound Stevie had never heard before in a dog, there was no sign of life outside either. The air was still, and no leaf moved. Moonlight caught on the barn roof and the spring pond and washed the grass of the back lawn with silver-green, unreal and soft, making it like some garden where feet had never yet walked. It was enclosed by the shadows that grew under the willow trees and in the orchard on the hill above. The great floodlights that watched over the Bane glowed dimly and yellow, as if a cloud or a patch of fog lay across that part of the mountain.

The Elephants had stopped. Their lights were on, but they were silent. Stevie had not noticed when they left off clanking their jaws and straining at their cables, but it must have been before Willy started up.

Nothing moved but Willy's shifting pale blur against the dark barn window.

"I wonder if there might be rats or something in the barn," Stevie worried. He wasn't sure whether rat bites gave dogs the plague or not. Or was it rabies?

He slipped from the window seat and tiptoed across to the hallway door. Turning the knob very slowly, he eased the door open and stuck his head into the hall. There was no sound from his aunt and uncle's room, and yet one of their windows opened toward the barn even more directly than the loft room's. He pulled the loft door to behind him and moved to listen at the girls' door.

A faint scratching noise met his ear. It scratched steadily for a moment or so and then paused as if something or someone were listening to be sure they had not been heard. After a few seconds it started up again. He turned the doorknob slowly—so slowly that he thought he would get a crick in the knuckles.

The room was very dark, as the moon hung high above the other side of the house and did not reach these windows. He could hear someone breathing quickly and shallowly somewhere close by.

"Miggle?" He made it scarcely a whisper. He felt along the wall for the bedpost.

"Yes. Here. Arthur?"

"No, it's me. Stevie. Where are you?"

She put out a hand. "What's going on outside?" she whispered.

"Nothing; but I think old Willy's got rats in the barn or something."

"No, it's something outside. Outside here. I heard it rustling around down at the bottom of the rose trellis just after he started barking; and it was coming up and I was afraid to look."

She was sitting bolt upright in bed, holding the walnut box in her lap. As Stevie's eyes grew more accustomed to the darkness in the room, he could see that his sister and Trish were awake, too, sitting up in the big double bed with the sheet wrapped around them so that only their eyes and noses looked out.

"You go scare it away, Stevie." His sister sniffled.

The scratching sound started up again. It came from the direction of the window opposite the door and sounded almost inside the room. Stevie looked around helplessly.

"I'll go get the baseball bat and Dub," he hissed.

"Here, use this," said Miggle, reaching under her pillow and pulling out a heavy long flashlight. She thrust the box under the covers and crawled out of bed. The younger girls had refused to budge, and she had been too frightened to go to the window alone.

"I'll come. We don't need Dub. Besides, it would take too long to wake him up."

Slowly, while Kit and Trish watched wide-eyed and breathless, they crept to the wall and then along it to the window. Stevie held the big flashlight like a club, and Miggle, her long braids undone, managed to look a little bit fierce for the benefit of her audience. The rose trellis was of course too flimsy to support a man, so she knew it wasn't a burglar; but after her fright in the chicken coop, she half wished it could be. Burglars were—well, human.

Stevie stopped abruptly. Miggle peered over his shoulder.

It was the weasels. One crouched on the outer window ledge, alternately scratching and biting at the base of the rickety old expandable window screen. It was trying to pull the outer portion of the screen far enough so that the entire screen could be pushed either into the room or down into the side yard. A second animal kept watch, its eyes shining angrily back and forth as its small head and long neck dipped and turned among the rose leaves.

Fumbling, Stevie snapped on the bright beam of the flashlight and fixed it on the two furious animals. One of them leaned downward and snarled as if in signal. Swiftly, Stevie handed the flashlight over to Miggle. With one hand he knocked the window screen out from under the sash, immediately slamming the window down with his other hand. The screen and the first weasel fell outward with a long clatter and a bump, while the second clung among the roses in surprise, baring his sharp little teeth in a hiss of fury and hatred. In the light that shone at him through the glass, his eyes were small shining points of red.

Miggle was shaking so with relief that for a moment the light wavered, dipping below the window sill, and in that moment the second weasel fled.

"Hoo!" breathed Stevie. "Boy, oh horsefeathers! Good old Willy-dog."

Miggle laughed. "He sure is. Golly, if he hadn't waked us up . . . " She could not finish for shivering. Stevie locked the window.

"What was it? Did it go away? What was it?" Loud whispers came from the big double bed.

Very quickly, there were four in the large bed, and there was much excited whispering.

"You know," Miggle said suddenly, "it *was* the box they were after." She padded back to her own bed and brought the box back, holding it tightly. "They *were*, you know. Just like in the chicken coop. I meant to tell you the rest of that, but I thought you all–that Dub would think it was silly. Not now. This key thing has something to do with the mountain, with Nũtayẽ. I know it has!"

In the chicken coop, she explained, the weasels had made no attempt to go after the chickens until after they were discovered. Somehow they had known that the box was in the hallway. They had been snuffling and scratching along the partition baseboard; and when the upper part of the door had opened, one had given a sharp cry, and all had streaked toward her.

"That's why you didn't come back down to the house for your dad?"

"Um hm. I was scared they might come out the hatch after me. It was only a funny feeling I had, and I thought you'd all think I was just imagining it, so I didn't say." She hugged the box. "But now I'm sure. And before it's too late, we've got to get it to Durwen and Maelin."

"Not tonight?" Stevie was alarmed.

"Golly, no. Even with moonlight the Wood must be black as pitch. I'd be scared spitless. Wouldn't you?"

"Well, it *would* be better in daylight." He tried not to sound too relieved. "Besides, there's a cloud or fog or something up on the Ridge, and the Elephants have stopped. In fact," he said, puzzled, "they stopped sometime before Willy started up. Do you suppose the fog could have come up out of Banebottom?"

She shrugged. "Clouds sometimes sit up on the Ridge. Or fog up by the dam. But I'll come look." She scrabbled awkwardly under her own bed for her slippers, clutching the box to her side with one arm.

"We'll come, too," whispered Kit. "I don't like it in here. It's too dark. I want to be with Stevie and Arthur."

In the end all four crept back along the hall and into the loft, the girls carrying pillows and the light blankets that had been folded at the bottoms of their beds. There was still no sound from Mr. or Mrs. Arthur. Not even the slamming of the window had wakened them, nor had it wakened Arthur. He did not move even when Kit climbed up on the bed. Trish curled up in the armchair. Miggle and Stevie sat in the two corners of the window seat, sharing between them a blanket over their feet.

A slight breeze had come up. The windows were the sort that cranked shut, but Stevie and Miggle left them open because these window screens were solid enough to be safe. They were metal-rimmed with a stubborn spring lock on the indoor side. They rolled up like blinds, following a track along the sides of the window frame, and could not be opened from outside. Usually, they could not be opened from the inside either. Pressing her nose against the screen, Miggle watched the back garden, the barn, and the hillside. Willy still stood at the dark barn window, a gray shadow. Fog was creeping down through the orchard. Otherwise, nothing moved.

Before long the fog had grown quite thick among the trees, and the barn became little more than a dim bulk off to the right. Stevie was nodding and both Trish and Kit had fallen asleep on the bed when Arthur, for no apparent reason, awoke at last. He sat up, squinted at them all, and rubbed his eyes.

"What's the matter? What's everybody in here for?"

He came to the window and sat in the middle, peering at the fog and listening wide-eyed to the whispered account of the weasels.

"Oh, come on! What would a bunch of weasels want with a box and a key to nothing, or whatever that thing is? I bet you had cookies or something in there, and they were just crazy hungry."

"We did not! They were not!" Miggle wriggled with frustration. "Why do you have to be so full of sour grapes? Don't you care about Nũtayẽ at all? We *know* the key—if that's what it is—has something or other to do with Nũtayẽ, and it must be horribly important. Just like I said, it was just asking to be found—and in spite of all the dumb things I did. Look at—at the arrow and that shiny rock in the pool, and then it comes bouncing all the way down the hill to plonk on top of the chicken coop when the Bane tried to swallow it!" She was scornful. "Do you think *that* was a coincidence? Some coincidence!"

Arthur shrugged. "Maybe so, maybe not. Heck, *I* don't know, Mig. Sometimes I think we're all just *thinking* Nũtayẽ and all that into being real, that we made it all up so we could fool around about defeating the Bane. I mean, like maybe there *are* caves up there and Káolin or Colin or whatever his name is does live there . . . but maybe they're plain old caves and people. Or maybe they're just fooling us about having been up there so long, and all that . . ."

He trailed off, seeing the growing distrust in their faces. He could tell that together, silently, they were agreeing to shut him out. He hastened to explain.

"No, no. I don't mean that's what I *really* think. When we were up there, I knew it was all true—that the Bane was a matter of life and death. With them everything was—was *more* of whatever it was: more beautiful or happier or more terrible. Then when we came away, everything was the way it ever was. I just don't understand how both can be—true." He wanted very much to make them understand but knew he was explaining himself badly.

"Look," he said. "If only one could be true, I wish it was them. Honest I do."

"You sound like a grownup," said Miggle coldly.

They might have argued further, but the fog had deepened and now pressed about the house, moving through the windows and into the room in wisps. The children cranked the two side windows shut. Arthur was working on the middle one when they heard Willy whining dimly, as if he were very far away.

Then they saw Periel, standing on the small landing outside the window, peering in past swirls of fog.

Chapter Fifteen

"Periel!"

Miggle's exclamation roused Trish and Kit, who sat up tousled and sleepy-eyed, undecided whether or not they ought to be frightened.

They saw a slight figure no taller than Miggle, garbed in a sleeveless blue dress, long and fastened at the shoulders with clips of gold or some like metal. Her hair was caught back in a long single braid, and it gleamed palely in the fog. The girls thought they had never seen anyone so beautiful. She beckoned urgently. The fog eddied about her.

"Aren't you going to let her in?" asked Trish.

The three at the window shook free of their surprise.

"Sure!" Arthur exclaimed. He swept the center window-seat cushion onto the floor and fumbled at the spring lock on the window screen.

"Just a minute. This thing's stuck again."

Miggle leaned over him to whisper through the screen, "Are we glad you've come! Did Durwen send you? I bet he hasn't guessed the best news yet. We found the box! But it isn't safe here. They keep trying to get at it."

Arthur freed the catch, and the window screen scritched noisily up its track. Nervously, the children all turned to listen into the darkness. All they needed was for Rover to wake up. Mr. and Mrs. Arthur could never sleep once he got going.

"All clear. Come on in." Arthur held out a hand.

But Periel shook her head and moved back from the window. She gave a nervous look over her shoulder and turned to them once more with distress and urgency on her small pale face. Putting a warning finger to her lips, she moved to the head of the steps and beckoned almost frantically.

The children did not like the look of the fog and were reluctant to go out into it. It was too thick. Yet there apparently was some urgent reason that they should put caution aside. Periel returned to the window, holding out her hands in pleading fashion.

"O.K.," said Arthur, taking a deep breath. "I'll go. There might have been an accident or something. The rest of you stay in, but leave the window open a crack and keep your eyes open. Where's that flashlight you had?"

Stevie passed it to him.

"Why doesn't she say anything?" Kit whispered. "Can't she talk?"

Arthur sat on the window seat and swung his legs out over the sill. Periel drew back, shook her head violently, and pointed over his shoulder.

"What? Who is it you want, then?" He brought his legs back inside and wriggled around to face the others. He

frowned. "I guess I won't do. She's been sent for someone special—Stevie, or maybe you, Mig. I wish they could wait. That fog is nasty."

Miggle pointed to herself questioningly and through the open window saw Periel nod excitedly and beckon once more.

"Me? Oh, Dub, hadn't I better go? I could take the box, and then we wouldn't need to worry about it any more. If the fog's too bad, I could stay in Nũtayẽ and sneak back down in the morning. Couldn't I?"

"Miggle? Please, Mig, don't go," Trish called softly.

But Miggle reached into the pocket on her dressing gown and drew out the long blue feather ribbon. With it she tied the walnut box securely, making a long loop that could serve as a handle. Climbing up onto the seat, she leaned out, offering the loop to Periel. But Periel refused it, moving aside and indicating that Miggle should step down to the landing and follow her.

It was awkward. Miggle ended in slipping the ribbon loop over her head so that the box hung like a great round locket bouncing against her breastbone. Then while she held onto the window frame with one hand, she gathered her nightgown and robe up around her knees with the other.

Stevie's nose was pushed against the window on the right. What had seemed the pressure of Periel's urgency now held some other quality, a cold weight that pushed against his mind and laid a chill upon his heart. He watched her face, now smooth and blank, as she saw Miggle reach one slippered foot down to the landing. There was a dullness behind her eyes, none of the shifting intensity of blue flecked or flashed with silver. His glance moved down her figure where she stood against the railing, half screened by the fog.

"Dub!" He snatched at his cousin's arm and pointed to the floor of the landing. The fog swirled only thinly there, so that the floorboards and the bottoms of the railing spokes were visible, faintly but clearly.

No feet small and richly shod stood upon that floor. No footprints broke the glistening fog-damp shine upon the painted boards. The image of Periel wavered dimly below the knees. It was clearly visible only where the fog was thick enough to mask the railing behind her. Something dark passed across the image, blurring the fairness of the Periel-face as it watched Miggle sliding down from the window sill.

Arthur moved as quickly as the alarm that spread through him. He reached out, grabbed Miggle around the waist, and pulled with all his strength.

"It's not her! It's not Periel!" he gasped as Miggle, surprised and angry, fought to break loose. Only by throwing himself backward off the window seat could he drag her free. She fell half on top of him, and her head hit the thinly carpeted floor with a painful thunk.

Stevie had begun cranking the window shut the moment most of Miggle was back inside the room. One slipper was caught as the window slammed, but as there was no longer a foot in it, he hurriedly poked it free and snapped the lock. He leaned his forehead against the cool glass. As he cranked, the fog had pushed in at him, seeming almost to hold the window back from obeying or to slow his hand upon the handle. The heaviness of air and of heart that had beat at him was the same that he had felt in that deep chamber of Nũtayẽ where the unlive power at the roots of the mountain was sealed beneath stone and sign. It pulled at something in you—he didn't know quite what—but it left him feeling very shaky in the knees.

Miggle was on the floor, crying in soundless gulping sobs and being petted and comforted by Trish and Kit. She kept trying to say something, but her indignation and the shuddering hiccuping sobs and sniffles prevented her from making herself understood, least of all to Dub, who seemed to be the object of her attention. He sat in a daze, the wind completely knocked out of him by having had all ninety pounds of Miggle land square on his middle.

When at last he did catch his breath, aided (or possibly delayed) by Stevie's helpful blows upon his back, Miggle had calmed down and was tearfully inspecting the scraped places on the backs of her legs. There was a nasty scratch down the back of one leg—on top of yesterday's brush burn. She looked up.

"Do—do you always h-have to be so darned rough? You could've just told me to come back in, c-couldn't you?" She sniffled again.

Arthur took a deep breath. "You wouldn't have come. That fog wasn't any plain old fog. Or even if it was, there was something else behind or in it. It made things—dim. As soon as I touched you, something—not a voice, but something in me—said, 'Let her go. You don't care. She has the box. It's her they want, not you. It's safer not to do anything. Besides, it's nothing to do with you.' " He scratched his nose, embarrassed. "And that made me mad. It was like somebody or something thought I was chicken."

"Well," said Miggle, truthfully but not too graciously, "I'm glad you weren't. But my head hurts awfully. And my leg stings."

Trish volunteered to look for the Merthiolate and Band-Aids in the bathroom cupboard and went off with the flashlight.

"What do you suppose she–*it* would've done if I had gone?"

Stevie turned from where he sat looking out the window. "You know, that's what was funny. Didn't you try to give her–that thing, I mean–the box? And it wouldn't take it? You know what I think? I think it wasn't real at all. It was kind of like . . . like an ottical . . . otticalusion."

"Optical illusion."

"Yes. Like that. So it was just there to make you bring the box. To the Bane, I bet."

Miggle shivered, touching the box. She unslung the ribbon from around her neck and rubbed her breastbone ruefully. "Boy, it gave me a bonk right there. I bet it'll be black and blue."

Arthur laughed painfully. "And you gave *me* a bonk right there. I'll be black and blue clear to my Adam's apple." He felt his ribs gingerly.

Trish returned with shushes and a bottle of antiseptic. While Miggle dabbed at her leg, Trish warned that Mrs. Arthur had heard her rummaging in the bathroom or seen the moving light under the door.

"I said I wanted a glass of water," she whispered. "So I ran the water a little while and took a drink. We'd better shut up and get back to bed or they'll come clear awake, and it's awfully late. The clock in the bathroom says two-thirty."

Arthur nodded. "We can't do anything more tonight, anyway. Tomorrow we'll take the key to Durwen first chance we get. The sooner the better." He went to the windows and looked out. "The fog's almost all gone, but keep your windows locked anyhow. And we'll leave both doors open into the hall."

He spoke with his old assurance, and the girls moved swiftly and silently to retrieve their pillows and blankets and slipped back to their own room. Very quickly the house settled into silence. In the barn a hoarse and tired Terwilliger settled down at last to sleep on a sweet bed of straw beside the puppy Trumpkin's box. The horses stood trembling until at last their heads nodded and they slept.

Chapter Sixteen

The next day was awful. It seemed that there would never be a chance to go up into the Wood. The family had been invited to Great-Aunt Margaret's in Colwyn, across the Ridge, for Sunday lunch. The animals had to be fed and watered, and everyone was to be ready to leave at ten-thirty. By hurrying with the chickens and gathering the eggs as quickly as she could, Miggle was able to manage a brief visit to Mr. Dekany.

"The mine?" asked Mr. Dekany. He looked at her sharply as he sucked the match flame into his pipe. "Hmm. Well." He puffed.

"Now you, my dear young lady, could not have been one of the mice sniffing around the entrance to my little hole in the hill the other day? Surely not. But so, I am forgetting! You have a curiosity about doors in hills, especially those which are meant to be shut. Hmm. Here, come do sit down. You fidget from one foot to the other until I forget what we talk about." He motioned for her to sit beside him on the back-porch steps.

"Yes, that is better. Now. First you must tell me why."

"Why?"

"Of course 'why'!" He waved his pipe at her. "You do not come in a rush through the vegetables to make only polite speech with old Michael Dekany. How is it even that you know something has happened to me there in the mineshaft? Hah? Tell me that. Only Mrs. Dekany has heard me speak of that."

Reluctantly, Miggle explained that she had heard it from friends who lived up on the Ridge. She had no idea how they had heard of it. They had not known exactly what had happened, and she was curious. She tried to shift the talk away from the folk.

"Why? Was it something dreadful? What did happen?"

Mr. Dekany rubbed his chin. "Hah. These friends of yours. Might one of them be about your size? Goldish red hair? Shy of being seen? One who leaves no footprints?"

Miggle hesitated. "It could be. Well, yes."

"Hmm. So I thought. And fond of eggs he is, too. He does not pay only social visits to your chicken coop and mine."

"But he always pays for things," said Miggle in alarm. "He always leaves something." How could she explain?

The old man nodded and watched her shrewdly. "Yes. And times there are when I have come home to find already my wood chopped or the chickens' floor cleaned. So I hold my tongue and perhaps—an absent mind, no doubt—I perhaps leave a jar of milk or a fresh-baked loaf here on these steps. This I was taught as a boy in my homeland: to ask no questions of these folk. It is not good to meddle with them. I tell you this to warn you; and I ask no more questions."

Embarrassed, Miggle nodded. Though she had promised not to talk about Nũtayẽ to anyone, she was disappointed that the only older person who had an inkling didn't want to hear any more. The folk had said that they and their kindred were feared and mistrusted. So they were, it seemed.

"You ask about this mine." Mr. Dekany pointed with his pipe stem to the shadow of its entrance in the bank under the eaves of the orchard.

"It was ten years ago, or twelve perhaps. Times were a bit hard, and I thought to bring out enough coal to sell, not only what was for ourselves. And so it was that I began to explore into the mountain to find where best it was to dig. None had gone so far in since the mines were abandoned. As I went further, the air grew heavy, and fearing it was foul, I went cautiously. There was, deep there in the earth, a sound. Not of proper digging, but a scrabbling, a brushing at the earth. And the walls dripped water, which lay on the ground in pools. Strange it was. Something filled me with such a dread! And so I went from there fast as could be, to come back with dynamite and long fuses. The roof I brought down in many places, so that now my little hole goes only back so far as one hundred feet. I dig now in little galleries off to the sides, scarce enough for our winter fires." He sighed. "A truly cold winter would finish it. But never have I regretted what I did. Some evil thing sought to be freed, and I must shut the door in its face, no?"

Miggle shivered. "Yes!"

Mr. Dekany pointed his pipe at her. "Think me a foolish old man if you wish. I imagined it, my wife says. But one does what it seems one must do, eh? Hah! Go away, go away!" He flapped his big hands at her. "It is too bright and fair a morning for such talk."

Mr. Dekany's story, when Miggle had repeated it to the other children, doubled their eagerness to reach Nũtayẽ with the key. The short trip to Colwyn and Great-Aunt Margaret's seemed more like seventy miles than seven, and the day seemed determined on passing slowly.

Great-Aunt Margaret loved to cook and she loved to talk. Between the two it was only rarely that the Arthurs succeeded in getting home to Ridgebottom Farm before five or six o'clock. The children worried away the middle of the day. Before lunch they explored a short distance down Lickpiddy Creek, halfheartedly looking to see whether they could find the old sealed-up stream opening that had once been a gate into Nũtayẽ, but they did not look for long. They hurried back to the village and Great-Aunt Margaret's kitchen, offering to help with setting the table, mashing potatoes, washing up pots and utensils almost before they had been finished with—anything they thought might speed up lunchtime.

Everyone wondered at them and smiled uncertainly. So sobersided and helpful? And very much like one ten-legged animal, they kept so much together. Trish and Kit stuck to Stevie like limpets, where usually they were off to themselves. Miggle, and Arthur, too, seemed to be at the center, and the busy, helpful swirl ended in impeding the preparation of the meal quite as much as helping it forward. Stevie picked up an iron skillet without a hotpad, promptly dropping it and scattering hot grease in all directions; whereupon he lavished a whole roll of paper towels upon wiping up the spattering. Miggle—or rather, the walnut box—broke one of Great-Aunt Margaret's Minton china cups. From the moment she had dressed, through breakfast and chores, in the car, and on through the day, Miggle had worn the box at her side in an aged shoulder-strap bookbag. The strap was mended with shoelaces and the bag part tied up with string. She had refused all pleas to take it off, and at every sudden turning in the close quarters of the pantry its swinging brought her poor aunt's hand to her throat in alarm. The broken cup—a very good one—was almost a relief to the dear old lady, for Mrs. Arthur promptly exiled the children to the living room, thanking them for their help.

Despite delays, lunch once served was delicious and undamaged: veal and mushrooms, mashed potatoes, buttered green beans, and for desert two meringue cakes topped with whipped cream and mandarin orange sections. After the meal Great-Aunt Margaret protested very earnestly that she really did not want any help with the dishes, and the afternoon visit did not spin on to its usual length. Mr. Arthur wanted to get home in time to get in touch with Mr. Padgett and, if necessary, drive on in to Kennington to confer with him.

The car nosed into the Ridgebottom driveway, and Mrs. Arthur got out to open the gate. Willy barked a welcome from the barn.

"What time is it, Daddy?" asked Miggle.

He looked at his watch. "Almost four o'clock. Three-forty-seven to be exact."

She opened her back door and jumped out. "Come on, we'd better hurry!"

The others crowded out after her. Rover, in the front seat, tried to climb over the seat and follow.

"Hurry? Where to?" Mr. Arthur leaned out of his window while holding Rover securely with his right hand.

"Up to see—Colin. We've just *got* to see him. It's about our key." She thumped the old bookbag.

"Mmm. Well, all right. But listen, Margaret: his family may not want five surprise guests on a quiet Sunday afternoon. Show the key to your friend if you must, but don't stay." He checked his watch again. "You be back by—let's see—five o'clock. Hear?"

"Yes, Daddy." She nodded, itching to be away.

"Good, then. Have fun." He slipped the car into gear and drove on through the open gate.

The children headed down the road at a good fast walk but were brought to a stop by Mrs. Arthur's call.

"Hoo! Where do you think you're going, milords and ladies?" She was standing on the bottom rung of the gate, riding it shut.

"To Colin's," Arthur called back. "Uncle Owen said it was O.K."

"Not in your good clothes, it isn't. That trucking road is dusty enough to give me another load of laundry even if you *aren't* tempted into bramble patches and the Run."

"But Daddy said we have to be back by five," protested Trish. The children wavered.

"We'll stretch that a bit. You run in and change. And, Miggle, one of you had better let Willy out. Your father's putting Ro—Morton down for his nap, but I have to pack up some pottery to take into Kennington tomorrow. Come along; the less you dawdle, the sooner you'll be on your way." She stepped from the gate, pushed it fast shut, and turned toward the house.

The children ran. For about five minutes there was a great slamming of doors, thumping of stairs, clattering of drawers, and thunking of shoes. Soon they were on their way again, this time by the shorter route across the meadow and through the Wood to the trucking road and the turning past the dam. Mrs. Arthur watched through the high basement window and smiled. There was something both fragile and tough to children running lithe-limbed through tall grass. She turned to her worktable and with a soft pencil began sketching a line of children. They would run around the rim of a grass-green bowl, she thought. She sat down to work it out and only then heard the unhappy barking from the barn.

"Oh, dear. They've forgotten to let Terwilliger out. I'll have to go up as soon as I finish this." She bent over the drawing.

Chapter Seventeen

Along the ancient road branching north along the dam the children searched vainly for the treeway leading upward to the green grass bowl of a meadow that lay below the entrance to Nũtayẽ.

"Did you say it was behind a fallen tree?" called Kit.

"Yes. You found something?" answered her brother.

"No. There's a log here, but it's only ferns all around."

"Yes. There were lots of ferns. I remember." Dub ran to look.

But it was not the place. There was no clump of tamaracks, no ravine, only the sloping hillside.

"It couldn't just get up and walk away. Could it?" asked Trish.

"Maybe we haven't gone far enough," said Miggle.

Arthur shook his head. "I don't think it was even this far. But I suppose we'd better have a look around that next bend just to be sure."

Around the next bend the old road itself gave out, spreading into a wide faint circle that must once have been a turn-around for lumber teams and wagons. Beyond were laurel thickets, wild strawberry, and a powdering of oak seedlings across the wide tree-shaded hillside. Nothing else.

They turned back, poking and peering along the uphill side of the road with no more luck than before.

"Whoa!" said Arthur at last. He brought the straggling line to a halt. "There's the turn down to the dam ahead. We've passed the treeway *again*."

"You don't suppose it *did* get up and walk away," said Miggle doubtfully.

"Don't be silly. Darn, I wish we'd brought Terwilliger. He found it the first time."

"I forgot. Mother told me to let him out, but I forgot."

Stevie looked thoughtful. "How did it go? 'Silver-eyed the dog alone can find the way–something something'? I bet it does mean we can't find it without Willy. We can't see it."

Arthur regarded him soberly. "Good for you. I forgot all about that. Káolin said they still had a way of keeping their entrance up above unseen. Maybe the same thing goes here. Maybe we ought to give up and go back."

Miggle protested. "We've just *got* to find it. They won't come looking for us because they can't know we've found the key thing." She looked around nervously, clutching the bookbag.

"And I don't want to spend another night all shut up in a hot stuffy bedroom sitting on this thing like a broody old hen," she added.

Arthur brought out a battered watch with the buckle part of the strap missing. It did not keep very good time, but he had brought it along so that they would not lose track of five o'clock when it came.

"We've got about five minutes before we ought to go back. What do you say we go over to Throne Rock and see if Káolin or anybody's been over there?"

"It was tomorrow he was going to be there. At three," said Stevie.

Arthur shrugged helplessly. "Anybody got a better idea?"

No one had. So, slowly, ill at ease, watching the Wood, they went.

The Wood was quiet and cool, and though sunlight broke through here and there in long slanting shafts to make patterns on the rock-strewn roadway, the splashes of light were as still as the leaves above. Only the motes of dust seen drifting through the bars of sunlight moved. At the forking of the road, the children could see down through the tunnel of arching trees into the glaring yellow and gray-green world across the dam. The trees at the water's edge seemed to droop even more wearily than they had the day before, and the shining face of the water was dulled as if it were a mirror some great hand had smeared with a dusty rag.

Up the south branch of the fork above the dam, the late afternoon sun was cut off by the swell of the climbing hills. The Wood here was more deeply shadowed, yet it seemed neither dark nor dim. As on the first day the children had come here together, all was fresh and clear, leaf and blade and stone. The Run splashed over rock and long-felled tree in a froth of white and slid across pebble and sand carrying downstream a leaf or sometimes a water beetle in its slow swirls. Its song among the stones was quiet—but oddly quiet, as if Run and Wood together were more awake than when leaf flashed or stones tumbled in spring flood: awake and listening.

At the round pond by Throne Rock, the listening silence was even deeper. Arthur waited until the others had gathered close before he spoke. He half expected his voice to ring out loudly among the trees, and so he whispered.

"What?" asked Miggle in a normal voice.

"I said, 'There's no one here.' Come on, let's beat it. It must be almost five."

"I guess we'd better. Darn!" She bent to fidget at her shoe.

"Won't we get to see the caves, then?" asked Trish.

Kit stood beside her, her disappointment as vivid as her freckles. "I've never been in a cave. Not even a little one."

"Tomorrow," Stevie promised. "Tomorrow afternoon. Only, you'd better call it a house around Aunt Vi and Uncle Owen. That doesn't sound as nutty. And the outside bit does look sort of house-ish."

"Come on, Mig," urged Arthur.

She sat down on the bank. "I've got a stone or something inside my sock. Just a minute." She took off the shoe.

They waited. Trish retied one of Kit's hair bows. Stevie fashioned a boat from two leaves and a thin twig and watched it ride the rapids from the pond to the deeper, swifter water below. Arthur climbed out to the seat in the middle of the rock dam and sat facing upstream. As he sat, listening, the Wood suddenly sprang into speech. The roof of leaves leaped into a wild rustling that swept up the hill like a sudden flight of birds. Water lapped high about the Throne. Alarmed, Arthur jumped from the seat, across the boulders, and to the bank. Miggle was just getting to her feet.

"Hurry! Get to the road and run!" He pushed her and urged the others ahead of him.

"What is it?" shouted Stevie above the rushing wind in the treetops.

"I don't know. But it's a warning, I think." He grabbed Trish's hand and pulled her along. "We're not going to stick around to see what for, either! That way–" He pointed downhill.

They angled down in the direction of the road in an attempt to shorten the distance to the dam. The way they had come had been carpeted with leafmold and wildflowers, but now, unexpectedly, they ran into a thicket of laurel.

"Around this way," called Stevie, moving back toward the Run. He pulled Kit in his wake.

But in a moment that way, too, was blocked–by a great looping curtain of wild grapevines that swung between the trees and out over the Run.

"No! Come back. It'll be quicker to cut uphill to the road," cried Dub. The Wood behind them was darkening, and he knew as surely as if the blowing trees had spoken it that they must get into the open. He herded the others before him.

"There!" The road lay across their path less than ten yards ahead.

"Oh, stop!" shrieked Miggle. The shoestring knotting the shoulder strap to the bookbag had parted with a snap, sending the bag rolling back down the slope.

Arthur swerved to keep from crashing into her as she wheeled to swoop after it. Turning, breathless, the others saw with dismay the drifts of fog that moved among the trees below. Red-faced and puffing, Miggle stumbled back with the precious bag clutched tightly under her arm. A tentacle of fog streamed swiftly after her, and Arthur felt a chill run through him as he put out a hand to her.

"Don't let's get separated," Stevie warned. He kept a tight hold on Trish and Kit. "Stay close."

They did not regain the road before the fog gathered to itself and encircled them. It was thick and cold, so thick that no one could see the other whose hand he held.

"Crumbuddle!" breathed Stevie.

"Miggle, where are you?" Trish whimpered, twisting around and out of Stevie's grip.

Stevie stopped. He tried to keep his voice calm. "Stay where you are, Trisha. Mig's right behind us. Don't move. If we split up, it'll be just what the old fog wants. It's after the box, not us really." His voice sounded as if he were speaking through thick folds of cloth.

"Please, Trish." Miggle was frightened. "Please don't move."

"I've got Miggle," said Arthur's voice. "Are you there, Trisha?"

"Y-yes?"

"You stay right there, and we'll latch on. You stick your arms out at both sides, O.K.?"

She sniffled. "O.K. Now what?"

"Swing them around like–like you were doing exercises. Not too fast, now." He inched forward, swinging his free hand back and forth. "Stevie, you and Kit stay put until we find her."

All five children concentrated on each other so fiercely that they offered no hold, no opening, to the heavy pressure of the fog pulling and pushing against their minds, driving insistently between them.

Trish squeaked. Arthur's hand had slapped against her own.

In a moment Stevie had caught her other hand, and the five gathered together into a close ring. Kit held Miggle's jeans pocket, for Miggle held the box in its bag tightly in her left hand, and Arthur held her right.

"We ought to hitch ourselves together," said Miggle. "It's too easy to let go if you got muddled or if you tripped and fell or something."

"With what? Shoelaces?" said Arthur. "Who's wearing a belt even?" The fog pushed.

"Don't be mean. Not now. I've got my blue belt. It's long. Here, let go my hand and hold my sleeve." She reached into her pocket and drew out the ribbon. The fog thinned slightly, and the others could see the movement of her hand and a shimmer of blue.

Fumbling awkwardly, she knotted one end of the soft ribbon around Arthur's left wrist and moved then to Trish, Stevie, and Kit. The fluttering end of the ribbon she gave to Arthur, who tied it tightly around her own left wrist, as she had done for the others. He had not thought it would be so long, but it left them freedom enough that they would not be treading on each other's heels.

"I feel kind of like a link of sausage," said Stevie. He gave a glimmer of a grin. For a fleeting second the others saw the glint of his red hair and the deep thoughtfulness in his blue eyes.

Arthur had not moved—except directly ahead—since

the fog had swept around them. He felt quite sure that he still faced uphill at right angles to the road. If they could get into the roadway, there was some chance of making their way out into the open at the edge of the dam. On the road they could feel their way along by the ruts. Yet as his mind turned outward, he felt the full weight of the fog pushing, thrusting against his will. Fears that downhill was up and uphill was down plucked at him. He hesitated but then stubbornly moved forward, moving his free right arm back and forth, a groping antenna. They crept ahead jerkily, uncertainly.

They had gone more than a dozen yards without meeting the road when the ground, unaccountably, began to fall away slightly before them. Though he still could see little beyond his outstretched hand, Arthur felt that the fog lightened ahead. They must have angled further to the right than he had supposed. The dam clearing must be in front of them. He lengthened his steps.

The younger girls, their usual chatter silenced by the strangeness of this gray world, stumbled—eyes screwed tightly shut—drawn forward by the wristlet of ribbon and the boys' shirttails, which they clung to fiercely. Stevie could hear his sister behind him, breathing in and out to the tune of "Kookaburra Sits on the Old Gum Tree" as fervently as if it were a spell to melt the fog away. Perhaps it was. He noticed that while he thought only about himself or his own feet, the fog seemed just a fog. But when he tried to turn his mind to what sort of fog it was, whether it came indeed from Banebottom, whether it might not be better for Miggle to be in the middle where he was, some dark anger flailed at him as if to beat his thoughts back to self and safety.

"Miggle?" It was difficult to get the name out.

"I'm O.K." Her voice came back, muffled, through the pressing grayness. "But it pushes at my back—the cold and wet. Can't you tell Dub to go faster? I'm freezing."

Arthur answered his call with, "It's clearing ahead, I think. We've circled down below the dam. We must've crossed the road back there."

They hurried in his wake.

The fog did indeed begin to thin—fading, slipping away from them, but lingering among the trees they passed. With relief Miggle saw that she was really tied fast behind Kit. In the fog she had been besieged by fears that she was in fact alone, tied at the end of a line that was slowly, surely being reeled in. Even now with a patch of blue sky ahead, she could not entirely shake free of the feeling. Around them fog shrank behind the hanging lacery of leaves and dark boles of trees only to close in once more beyond the edges of their vision. The illusion was that the branches, the trees themselves, were opening a path through the fog for them. Stevie's sharp-eyed curiosity strove to focus clearly on tree and branch; and though they seemed to bow and beckon, he was sure they remained stock-still, unmoving.

"Where are we going? We can't be going right," said Miggle nervously. The ground had once more bent upward beneath their feet.

They came from under the canopy of unmoving leaves into the still sun-washed sky. The last film of gray shrank back among the trees, and the children saw with bewilderment that they stood high on the very lip of the Bane. Below and away rolled the wide road-rutted benches, the bitter canyons, and the gaping jagged teeth of the stripping. Far beyond its lowest reaches in the late afternoon haze, there could be seen the tip of the tall fir tree in the Arthurs' side garden.

Arthur backed away from the steep edge, herding the others.

"How in heck did we ever get up here? How did we get across the Run? My feet are bone dry."

The others looked at their shoes in vague puzzlement. How could they have come so wrong? Stevie and Miggle exchanged a look over Kit's head, and both nodded when a half-understood explanation dawned in Arthur's dark eyes. They had been nipped at and harried, headed off and herded here as neatly as a flock of sheep with a sheep-dog snapping at their heels.

"We daren't cut across," warned Arthur.

Miggle turned back to the Wood at a run, skirting along a root-tangled bank, pulling the others after her.

"Oh, if *only* we had brought Willy!" she panted.

They had not looked to the fog when they came out under the sky. Now it took shape in front, around, behind them: fingers reaching after them, winding them once more in a cold clasp. The children stopped, dismayed. Then they stumbled on, striking down the slope and northward. The Run would surely take them to the dam if the road eluded them.

Yet time and again they were drawn back in tighter and tighter circles to the Bane. Each time the sunshine on the far trees above the Arthur orchard seemed to glow more warmly and the air sparkled, bringing the ancient fir tree and the welcome roof more temptingly near. Secret voices said to each of them, "Cut across. It is so close. See how near the road lies below, ready to lead you out through the Wood and home." Each time, they fled—until their fear and weariness changed to anger and frustration. Then the power that drew them no longer sought to tempt or confuse but to drive them as sheep before the ravening wolf. Ranging in circles around them as they ran, the children heard the padding, rustling passage of animals. This was what Arthur had feared from the first, and in the fog the noises turned them this way and that in terror. The snarls and hissing—even a long, heavy rumble Arthur could or would not put a name to—mounted, all the while unseen. The ribbon of children streamed once more to the brink of the Bane and wavered there, ready to plunge down the bank of crumbling shale.

Terwilliger barked. Somewhere in the Wood he bayed, sounding loudly on their trail.

"Willy! Mother's let Willy out, and he's come for us!" cried Miggle.

There was a scuffling in the undergrowth as their pursuers faltered and fled. Arthur guessed that they must have been for the most part the weasels or ferrets, though even a bobcat might think twice before facing a furious dog. That sound of the heavy shuffling body and deep rumble he put down to his own imagination.

Once more groping their way into the Wood, the children called long and loudly, but Willy seemed not to hear. The fog clung about them, and as he listened to the baying of the dog upon the hillside, Arthur guessed that their voices were muffled—possibly shut off altogether from reaching beyond the unnatural fog. The mist could not reach far from where they walked at its center, for when they had poised in the open above the Bane, they had seen it shrink from them in obedience to the will that directed it.

"So if we stay put," Arthur explained, "he'll find us

faster. He must be following our trail around and around. Listen!"

"Poor Willy. His nose isn't awfully good even on an easy trail," said Miggle shakily. She wiped her forehead with the back of her hand. The demanding pull upon her heart and feet had suddenly lessened. The mist drew back from among them as if it, too, listened for the loping dog, but warily.

The children stood close together. As Willy's urgent bark circled closer, they saw the angry fog grow pale and motionless. When at last he nosed happily into their midst and led them easily to the road and the dam beyond, they looked back to see that their moving prison was still and sullen, scarcely broader than the length of their soft blue lifeline.

Trish and Kit smeared at their teary faces.

"Is *that* where we were? That little patch?"

Arthur bent down to give Willy a hearty kiss full on his damp nose and was promptly whipped away over the breast of the dam and down to the county road at the end of the flashing ribbon of children Miggle drew behind her. She would not stop to untie the knots until she came with her following to rest at the sun-porch door.

Mrs. Arther stood there smiling. "I thought Willy would bring you home," she said.

Chapter Eighteen

"Mother isn't back yet, and it's almost two-thirty. What are we going to do?"

Miggle sat in the wicker swing on the front porch, where she could see the road as it passed out of the trees on the near side of the Run. An empty truck clattered past, heading for the turn-off.

Arthur sat on the steps. "When does she usually get back if she goes into town?"

"Before this." She was worried. "Before time to put Rover down for his nap. He won't stay put if Trish or I do it. If she goes in with Daddy like today, she usually comes on the first bus after lunch. That's the one that went past an hour ago. Oh, I wish we could go! I don't want to go up in the Wood late in the afternoon. It feels safer when the trucks are still going in and out. And besides, Káolin will think there's no news and go back to Nũtayẽ." The box lay in her lap. She was mending the strap on the bookbag.

Arthur watched the road. Two heavily laden trucks

turned out of the Wood onto the county road and rumbled past the house. Whatever doubts he had felt about the wisdom of joining with the folk had been forgotten when the dangers of that other world had crossed into his own. The not-Periel, the fogs, Mr. Dekany's tale—and, above all, the perilous power of the Bane to bend other wills to its own—all these had made fearfully clear that if he closed his eyes and ears to that darkness, its movements into the sunshine from the depths where wisdom had sealed it would be the freer. And he would be shut out—"dead" like the captured pawn in a chess game—held aside while the others moved freely in the patterns of their natures: Miggle, muddleheaded but yet single-minded, Stevie clear-eyed and singlehearted. Then there was Dub for double, he thought wryly. It *was* like a chess game—or *fidchell*, he thought ruefully, remembering—but one where loss was more than a word and a passing regret. To stand aside and watch was—every bit as much as to make things happen—a choice you were stuck with.

He stood up. "We'll just have to take Rover with us. Where is he?"

"Out back with the girls, I guess. But he can't walk that far. He's too little. And he weighs a ton if you try to carry him."

"So we'll take turns. You get him and I'll help round up the others. We haven't got much time. Káolin might not wait."

Miggle fastened the buckles on the bag. "Why don't we take Merrylegs? Rover could ride in front of me, the way he does with Daddy."

Arthur brightened. "Do you think we could take Duke

and Bobble, too? It would be a lot faster on horseback. And safer, too. If we ran into trouble, they'd be good to have along." Horses were so reassuringly large.

Miggle clapped with delight and slid from the swing. Káolin would be surprised! She swung the new-mended shoulder strap over her head so that the bag hung at her side, leaving her arms free, and then went in search of Rover. Then with Trish she set about pulling and coaxing the horses to the hitching rail at the top of the barnyard to be bridled. They had not been ridden for a week and were in a mood to play tag. Time was short when the gate swung open and the procession moved out with Willy trotting at its head. Kit rode behind Stevie on the palomino Bobble, and Arthur took Trish up behind him on Duke. They rode easily, without saddles, on the broad backs. The basset puppy, short-legged Trumpkin, pressed his nose against the dog-run fence and whimpered to see them go. Arthur had drawn the line at being seen on horseback wearing a basset hound in a pack basket.

Out on the road the trucks approaching them slowed, and men with worn, haggard faces smiled to see the children pass, their bright shirts fluttering banners in the flaring sun. " 'Tis good to see there's yet some without cares," said one, sighing to himself half bitterly. "But it ain't right they should get too near them diggin's. It's a nasty place. Downright creepy up there today, like thunder hangin' over it."

Káolin felt the threat in the air more keenly. Another few moments and he would have turned back to Nũtayẽ, for this new anger in the air dismayed him. None of the folk had come this way on the day before. They had spent the day in the woods and meadows on the far side of the Ridge, gathering grasses and herbs for the floors and stores of Nũtayẽ. They had returned at nightfall, but no rumor had reached the window over the Wood of the power that had been loosed against the children. Káolin stood upon the stone seat in the middle of the stream, his keen eyes fixed where, beyond the fluttering of many leaves, the old road breasted the dam. Not even the Eagle of Gwernabwy could see more sharply from so far.

He was startled at what he saw. He passed a hand across his eyes and stared again in wonder. Then with a leap he was on the bank and flashing through the Wood like the flicker of a shadow.

"What has happened?" he cried down the green-roofed way as he ran.

The three horses stood in the bright sunshine at the water's edge: one white, one golden, and one red. The children sat dumbly, marveling at the joy they saw in Káolin's face. As he regarded them, he seemed to grow taller and brighter, as if he were a lamp at last unshaded.

Arthur slid from Duke's back. He held a stout willow staff, a straight branch rudely trimmed and crowned with silver-green leaves.

"Can you take us to Nũtayẽ? Right away? The Wood isn't safe. We can tell you about it as we go. We tried to come yesterday but couldn't find the way."

"You see," said Miggle, "we've found my treasure, and they're after it."

"They?" Káolin regarded them with puzzlement and then a dawning understanding. "I see, though but dimly. Come. Save your tale for Nũtayẽ. Follow me now to the treeway, and then I shall go on ahead. I would not have my folk miss seeing your coming. There is a wonder in it you cannot guess."

So it was that they went up through the Wood, Arthur and the dog Willy following Káolin and the horses stepping after. Miggle, whose long braid had come undone, tied her blond hair back with the blue ribbon. Trish, pale with excitement, sat the tall red horse alone. Stevie and Kit came behind on golden Bobble.

As they rode up the ancient green aisle of beeches, the folk came from Nũtayẽ to meet them. They gathered in the green bowl at the crest of the hill and parted like grass under the wind's feet so that the boy and dog and the riders could pass to where Rhelemon, Garym, and Túdual stood with Durwen and Maelin. "So it is! So it is!" murmured Rhelemon, shaking her head as at a marvel.

For what the folk had seen was a scene from an ancient tale: a dark youth with a silver-crowned staff and a silver-eyed dog leading a fair-haired lady and a sleeping child on a milk-white mare and a company after them, garbed alike in blue and green—a girl-child riding a red horse and two of their own kin on a golden.

"Orin and his hound bringing Argána and their children out of the sea into Prydein! And Ywen and Aderyn!" The murmur ran around the company. "And see! Argána bears something at her side." The voices rang like bells. "The key? Does she bring the key?"

The cousins faltered as the soft voices swept around them. They were bewildered at the names bestowed upon them and the joy in the fair bright faces. Arthur caught sight of Durwen at the foot of the winding path to Nũtayẽ and moved forward, leading Merrylegs. The others

followed. Trish and Kit were lost in wonder, and Rover, awakening from his drowsing, was so quiet that Miggle wondered even more. He clutched at Merrylegs' mane, leaving Miggle free to unclasp the bag and draw out the walnut box.

Maelin reached up her hands to take it.

"Why do they say, 'Is it the key?' " Miggle asked. "How did you know?"

"Because," answered Durwen, accepting the box from his lady, "your coming upon the hill in this fashion has seemingly unraveled the riddle. It tells us that the old song which we told you of was of the past as well as the future."

"I don't understand," said Arthur. "How do you mean?"

Rhelemon smiled at him, green youth springing in her age-old eyes, and began to sing. The horses stood spellbound, and it seemed the trees bent to listen:

"Brindle dog and darkling child
Shall find the way within the Wild.
  Stone and feather fast en-isled!
Silver-eyed the dog alone
Can find the way beyond the Throne,
  To the feather and the stone.
The Morning Star shall ride the hill
To turn the waters to her will.
  Stone and feather, gem and quill!
Three the gates where one before,
Then seven the streams, one the door.
  Stone and feather bound no more.
When over treetops coracles sail
To free the Folk, unstay the tale,
  Stone and feather shall not fail!"

"I have known these verses from my childhood." She laughed. "And never did a one of us guess that it was a reminder of the ancient tale of Orin and Argána. She was often called Morning Star. Her husband Orin led her one dawning back out of her father Buan's kingdom in the sea. She was fair beyond the telling, and to those along the shore it seemed the morning star was caught in the net of her golden hair."

"And the others?"

"Her son she bore before her and her daughter rode behind. And with them came Aderyn and Ywen, friends to Orin from among our own kindred. Their horses were white and gold and red." She smiled upon Stevie and Kit. "Red-gold hair and wild blue eyes in children whose fore-folk come from Cumbrie! Who knows? Perhaps the long years unwoven would tell that we are kindred indeed."

Durwen held the walnut box up to Miggle. "There is some cunning in the craft of this box that I cannot master in my eagerness. Will you open it for us?"

Arthur lifted Rover down, and Periel and Meruel took him aside to play.

Miggle opened the box and held up the key thing.

"It must be—surely it is Argána's key!" breathed Maelin. The company sighed like a breeze in the rushes.

"Put it back in the box," warned Durwen suddenly. "We must not linger here. If Argána's key is found, it must to Nũtayẽ. Not even this our hidden Wood is safe."

The folk streamed upward through the Wood, a wind among the branches. The horses, following, were sure-footed and fleet as yearling colts. The children felt joy and strength leaping within their mounts and laughed. Only Miggle was sad as she leaned forward to lay her cheek on Merrylegs' neck, for the horses were old and she was afraid they might break their hearts in joy and obedience. But they came to the top without harm and through the high hedge of laurel into the meadow by the gate of Nũtayẽ.

The horses were stabled in the threshold room. The trestle table and chairs were moved, and the floor was strewn with fresh grasses. Willy and several of the company remained with them. It had been many long years since the folk had spoken with and cared for horses—except for chance meetings in lonely meadows—and they joyed in their dark eyes, velvet noses, and begging caresses. Much speech and many broken oatcakes passed between them.

Through the great gates and down the long stair, the greater part of the folk gathered where the children sat around the raised hearth. There, as the key was passed from hand to hand, the children told of the repeated attempts made against it and their apparent source in the Bane. Miggle repeated Mr. Dekany's tale. Durwen seemed to regard all this as confirmation of the identity of the key.

He explained. "According to the old tales, Argána—unbeknownst to King Buan her father—brought with her from the kingdom under the sea one of that kingdom's greatest treasures, the key to the waters. It had come to the King through Argána's mother. With this key he had loosed the waters upon the kingdoms of Teithi Hen, of Helig ap Glannawg, and of Rhedfoe ap-Rheged, sinking their towers and steeples beneath the sea. By her theft Orin's kingdom was saved from a like fate, and the key became the chief treasure of his house. Through Argána's wisdom it was seldom used and jealously guarded against those who were sent from time to time to attempt its restoration to King Buan. What became of it in the ages after their passing was never known. It seems clear now that it was brought across the sea and put to some use here."

"I see," said Arthur. "I mean, I think I do. You think that the song says that the key has something to do with freeing you from the Bane?"

Durwen's eyes sparkled. "Yes, by loosing the waters on it!" He looked to Maelin, Garym, and the others to find in their delight a sign that their thoughts had run in the same path as his own.

"Stone and feather: that is us, for the green jade and the feather are our signs," he said. "Some of the song remains dark, but one thing at least is sure: there is only one old river passage which could be said to hold seven streams. It is the old riverbed which branches from the chamber below which the dark depths are sealed. Once the river flowed into the sunlight through six welling springs and a falling stream . . ."

"Across the Bane!" said Stevie, sitting up electrified.

"Across the Bane." Durwen nodded. "Down through the Wood now uprooted. It can flow again to cleanse the festering wound, the anger that spreads in the flesh of the mountain."

"Golly," breathed Miggle. "If it was waterlogged, they couldn't do any more stripping, could they?"

Túdual raised a warning hand. "Go softly, my friends. First the gap must be closed. The dark lake where that world of shadows touches upon this world of sun and living things must first be sealed. Nothing will be gained—only changed—if the greedy and unthinking men with their innocent pawns are driven away. The naked power of the shadow will draw some other tools to work its will."

"But if Banebottom is stoppered up and the river is sent into the Bane, won't it make another dangerous lake or send floods of mucky stuff all down the hill?" Arthur's practical question dampened the enthusiasm of the company, for, of course, though Nũtayẽ would be freed, the Arthur farm would be endangered in such a case.

"Anyhow," said Miggle, "how can my key change the way a river goes?"

"There: the child comes to the point you have all leaped over." Rhelemon shook her head. Her voice more than the others was a clear shimmer in the air. "Hopes raised too high shatter more grievously if they fall. First we must find the lock which will fit such a key. That it is Argána's key I have no doubt. The metal is *findruin:* silver and gold hardened with some other ore. We have lost the art of its making but still have some few ornaments fashioned of it. This sign on the haft I take to be some sign of the morning star, for I have seen such a figure on one of the star charts among the books of Nũtayẽ. The shape of the wards—what do they remind you of?" She held up the key.

Miggle shook her head.

Stevie furrowed his brow. "A starfish? From the sea! What do you know!" He brightened. "It *means* water, then? But then, I bet I know . . ."

"Yes?"

He told them of seeing the sea-star sign somewhere in the chambers beyond the river bridge. Immediately, Durwen rose to send some of the folk to the storerooms for torches and others to run ahead kindling lamps in the passages. Túdual, Garym, and Rhelemon went as far as the Window Hall, there to sit among their books and puzzle what might be the full meaning of the ancient song. There was still much that was unclear. There, too, Arel and Briallen played under the crystal flowers with a sleepy Rover. The other children were swept along with the folk down the stairs and paths to the river level. Trish and Kit were helped along by many friendly hands, for they were so absorbed in all they saw that they took little care for where they stepped.

At the head of the long river caverns, a string of the shallow oval boats was drawn from their moorings under a low overhang of rock. Three were loosed and brought to shore. Durwen stood in the prow of the first, taking Stevie with him. As the boats filled, lights were set afloat as before, and torches set in tall standards were fixed in brackets along the sides, one between each two oarsmen. The flotilla moved swiftly into midstream and went gliding through the pinnacled halls. They lit the darkness like a slow shower of stars passing down the night sky. Eirin in song took up the verse of the old riddle, and Káolin answered with the refrain. Soon others joined in, and the notes rang among the shadowed columns along the banks.

"Three the gates where one before,
Then seven the streams, one the door.
Stone and feather bound no more!

When over treetops coracles sail
To free the Folk, unstay the tale,
Stone and feather shall not fail!"

In the second boat Miggle turned excitedly to Maelin. "This boat? Is this what you call a coracle?"

"Yes. Why do you ask?"

"The song! We're kind of riding inside the song, aren't we? Aren't we still high above most of the Wood?"

Maelin was startled. "So we are. I had thought the verse might have something to do with the tale of Argána. For long years men could sail across the kingdoms the sea had taken and, looking down onto the treetops and towers, hear bells ringing still." She nodded thoughtfully. "If you are right, it must mean simply that we will ride, as now, on our way to free the waters. We must ask Durwen. I had hoped it might. . . . But no mind, it is best not to build your bridge before its stones are quarried!"

She would say no more, but Miggle wondered whether she—and perhaps others of the folk—had hoped one day to be sailing over seas they knew, beginning a new voyage over the path from which their first had strayed.

In the chamber across the bridge, lights moved along the walls. Many hands groped along stone surfaces smooth and rough and among clusters of stony flowers. Stevie was confused, for nowhere did his eye meet the sea-star sign. The high spirits of the company began to wane in the heavy air, and he grew nervous. Durwen, seeing this, spoke calmly and retraced with him the steps he had taken two days before from the time when he had stepped from the boat. Just when Stevie was most despairing, he found it. He had climbed down several ladder rungs into the deep passage leading to the Chamber of the Seal, and as he looked up past Arthur's tennis shoes, it sprang into view on the wall facing him. It was at the knee level of those who stood above and was overhung by a small projection of stone, which hid it from the view of anyone standing in the upper chamber itself. A deep, small hole in the rock wall, it was shaped exactly like the star end of the key.

Káolin gave Stevie a hand back up, and the entire company gathered around as Durwen drew Argána's key from inside his wide sleeve.

"Stand well clear of the old stream bed," he warned. "And of the bridge, too. Back against the wall will be safest. We know not what this key may do. We must not fully loose or shift the waters now, yet I would know

something of how the key works. Our plans depend upon our knowing."

Stooping, he inserted the key in the hole. It slipped in easily. The lights trembled and no one breathed. Very slowly, he turned it one half turn. No seam was visible in the rock around the keyhole, yet Arthur thought some section of it must have moved, for the key turned freely.

For a moment nothing happened. Durwen turned the key further. Then there was a great rumble. The churning of the water where it poured into the deeps grew more violent. The froth made seeing difficult, but dimly a slab—a great tongue of rock—could be made out at the level of the channel bottom as it slid from behind and beneath the bridge. Thrusting through the water, it passed over the great hole into which the stream had plunged for long ages, sealing that hole fast shut. The water, shut out from its accustomed path, poured over the slab and into the old dry deep-cut bed. There it swirled angrily down through the shaft to the Chamber of the Seal. Where Stevie had clung not five minutes before, the river whirled out of sight.

"Quickly! Turn it back!" urged Maelin.

Durwen, shaking off his amazement, did so swiftly. The great tongue of rock drew back, and the water returned to its former course.

Under their feet they felt a trembling deep in the hill. The torches guttered, and the excited talk among the children and the folk faltered in the rush of reaching fear and black anger that smote them. It blew up from the chamber below and throbbed upward through the heavy fall of water.

"Let us to the boats," commanded Durwen. "And quickly. We have found what we hoped for and more. But I fear that in the finding our enemy may be warned. In my eagerness I had not thought, but I have told it that the children have reached us with the key, and I may have betrayed the measure of our strength. Quickly, to the boats!"

Chapter Nineteen

Above in the Window Hall, the bright chamber of grottoes, Rhelemon, Túdual, and Garym watched at the window on the Wood. When voices announced the appearance of Durwen and his company at the head of the curving stair, Túdual closed the window with a touch, Rhelemon drew back the heavy curtain, and they stepped out into the rose and gold light of the main chamber. Alarm crackled in the air.

"What has happened? Did some ill befall you on the waters? There is mischief afoot in the Bane—much dust and the cries of men—but we could make out nothing of what had befallen."

The three elders saw with dismay the thought that flashed behind Durwen's eyes: that their doings by the bridge must be the cause of whatever storm raged in the Bane.

"My wits lagged in this." He shook his head ruefully. "We found the place where the key was used, and, in my eagerness, I turned the key too far, for one brief moment closing off the weight of water which has so long poured into the caverns of the unlive realm below. For scarce three heartbeats the river ran instead down the passage to the hill above the Bane."

The children were forgotten as the folk debated what was best to do. They fell into a speech that rang like music on the ear but which was meaningless to the children and unlike anything they had ever heard before. Trish and Kit grew restless, and the others became increasingly uncomfortable as they realized that the talk was much concerned with them. From time to time a speaker would glance their way.

Arthur moved to the recess where the window was. He could not find the knob that opened the shutters. Behind him he heard the soft clash of curtain rings on metal and, turning, saw that Rhelemon had followed, drawing the draperies shut behind her. He was both pleased and a little afraid, dismayed by the sense of distance and hidden depths that marked all of the folk. Even when they laughed or teased, it colored their laughter with a richness come of remembering. It was as if for them no joy was new, none held surprise—which newness often is the thing men chiefly seek—but as if each joy were an old friend well met. Of Rhelemon all this was so; only more so. To Arthur it seemed, when afterward he tried to put words to it, that being near enough to touch her was like being on the edge of far places and further times. If you went too close, you might lose your footing in here and now.

He had never seen her so near as when she reached past him to touch the spring he could not find. She and the brothers Túdual and Garym moved in a world aloof even from most of the concerns of their sons and daughters and the younger folk of Nũtayẽ. They kept to their books and the shadows of the caves or the eaves of the close-by Wood—or had done so until the Bane drew them back into the waking world.

"We draw the curtain so that no glimmer of our lamps should chance to catch a curious eye in the Wood or on the far hills," she explained as the leaves of stone opened upon the slopes below.

"You cannot see from here whether the water Durwen loosed has made its way past the fall of rock which blocked the main passage to the east," she continued in answer to his unspoken question.

Arthur looked back, startled. She had drawn her shimmering black cloak around her, and her silver eyes looked almost to be seeing through the bones of the hill below.

"That's what I was wondering," he said. "If it just leaked out, instead of sloshing down into the Bane, maybe it wouldn't be noticed?"

Miggle slipped in under the heavy curtain. Rhelemon made room for her at the window but did not take her eyes from Arthur's face.

"Perhaps. If fortune holds and the omen of the song is fulfilled, we are safe. We will wait only for the news you say your uncle thinks is sure: the choking and covering over of the dark lake so that it can no longer suck at the hills and at men's hearts. Then Durwen purposes to free the waters with Argána's key. This troubles you? Come, say your thoughts." She watched him remotely.

He stammered. "It—it's just what I said before. Won't that wash muck into the streams? It's sure to end up making a monster lake down in the bottoms where the road goes. They won't be scared into filling any more than they have to—just where the water is now. More water would make it almost as bad as Banebottom." He felt her keen glance. "Well, not as bad as all that, but ugly and unsafe," he amended.

"But *we* would be safe. Is that what you are thinking? There is truth in this. Yet for the streams and farms, it is an evil far less than that now brewing. The others debate this now. For myself, I would have them wait until we are forced to act, on the chance that some better way will present itself. All along it has seemed that there was some purpose working in wood and stone and water, as if the mountain itself labored to protect us. You yourselves have seen the care it took to bring the long-lost key to light. The mountain's daughters move and speak, though they have neither tongues nor feet."

" 'The mountain's daughters'?" said Miggle. "But I made that up, didn't I?"

"Did you? Perhaps. Or maybe your heart heard that tongueless speech."

The two children were silent.

Rhelemon gazed out across the Wood. Dust still hung over the Bane.

"But young Arthur has other fears than this," she mused. "It is perhaps as well that they are not spoken. You must trust us whether you will or no. We do not only debate the safety of our mountain prison. Water can flow more ways than two. Yet I think we will prove true to your help and trust."

She would say no more. Silently, she closed the window and pulled the curtain to one side, indicating that they should rejoin the others.

* * *

Up in the threshold room Willy and the horses greeted the returning company with wagging tail and soft snorting nickers.

"Káolin and Illurin will show you to a safer pathway home than the one you know," said Durwen. "It will take you north, circling wide and coming to the road south of the great yellow barn."

"The Bakers'." Miggle nodded.

"Until it is known what happened this afternoon in the Bane, we will all do well to keep wide of it. If you have news or wish to come to us tomorrow, come to the Wood behind the yellow barn. We will set a watch for you there."

Once out and riding under the green-leaved sky, Trish and Kit found their lost tongues and poured out questions, exclamations, and excitement in a rush of words. When one ran out of breath, the other took up without, as Stevie teased, a lost mini-second.

"There's one thing I'd like to know myself, though," he said. "What was all that talk about? I listened so hard that Káolin laughed—said I looked like a baffled groundhog chewing away at my lip. I couldn't make head nor tail of it except for our names and some of the others'. Toward the end it got high and soft and sad, almost like music. They kept saying 'Tirnannog' or something like that. What do you suppose it was about?"

"'Tirnannog'? Wasn't Tir na'nOg the land they were looking for when they sailed from the old country?" asked Miggle, remembering the longing look in Maelin's eyes.

"Maybe," said Arthur. "I don't remember that. But I bet it's what they're thinking of. 'Water can flow more ways than two,' Rhelemon said. You heard how cautious she was: things better left unsaid and all that."

"What are you getting at?" said Stevie, flapping his knees against Bobble's barrel ribs, urging him up even with Duke.

"Well," said Arthur slowly, "if the key works the way I think it does, they have a way out of the mountain to the sea. But if they take it, if this Tir na'nOg means that much to them, it leaves the Bane free to spread its poison any old way it wants."

He explained. If—and it seemed possible—the heavy tongue of rock that thrust along the bottom of the stream bed were to reach only ten or so feet further than they had seen it move, it could close off the Chamber of the Seal as well. If it covered that shaft passageway, the stream would be turned into the path that led westward down long falls, through the jewel-like caverns Káolin had told Stevie of. If there was a way to get the boats through the passage and down past the falls, the crest of water could carry them out to the stream that wound through the Colwyn meadows.

"But that's Lickpiddy Creek," objected Miggle. "It's too shallow."

"The banks are high. With all that water from the underground stream, it would be a regular river. Straight sailing all the way to the Monongahela."

"*They* can't know that. They don't know it would lead to the sea."

Stevie interrupted. "No. Arthur's right. You remember that batch of old road maps you said got pinched before your dad could throw them away? Well, they're on a shelf with a lot of books in one of those little side rooms—grottoes or whatever you call them."

This news depressed Arthur even more. "Rhelemon said we would have to trust them," he said glumly.

The children could imagine, even if only dimly, what a hard choice the folk would have. They rode on in silence, the horses treading lightly, threading their own way downward through the trees.

"Hi! Hoo there! Where on earth have you been?"

The voice hailed them as they rode out of the open wood south of Bakers' barn. It was Mrs. Arthur. She was in the car and leaned across the seat to call to them as they came onto the road.

"What? Oh, we've been up visiting Káolin. Giving the horses a stretch," said Miggle, wrestling to keep her hold on a Rover suddenly awake and fighting to get down.

Mrs. Arthur laughed. "Hold on. I'll take the wriggleworm off you hands."

She pulled ahead and parked on the verge of the road.

"Mr. Padgett is coming out to dinner, so your father gave me the car for some errands. He'll come with Mr. Padgett. I'm sorry to be so late, but I had dozens of little things to attend to, and they always seem to take longer if you don't have to worry about catching a bus. Come along, Morton. Hup! You hadn't been riding on a gee-gee in a long time, had you? He hasn't had a nap, I suppose?" She addressed this last to Miggle.

"He's been awfully good, though. And he did sleep some. He hardly said a word while we were . . . visiting."

Mrs. Arthur and Rover got into the car.

"Colin's mother is going to think you're awful nuisances, tracking up there every day. Couldn't he come down to the farm sometime to play?"

Stevie choked. Kit and Trish smothered giggles.

They all sobered quickly, however, at Arthur's answer. "Probably not," he said, looking at Miggle. "We're afraid they're going to move away."

Glumness descended again.

After dinner Arthur, Miggle, and Stevie sat listening to Mr. and Mrs. Arthur and the lawyer.

"We both missed some fireworks, Owen," Mr. Padgett said, putting down his coffee cup. "I thought I would see how the land lay with Minshew before I went to Judge Carsten. I let it fall—very innocently—in the County Recorder's office this morning that we intended bringing an action against Minshew Coal. When I got back to my office, I sent young Jamieson home to get into some old clothes. Told him to come out here to the stripping. You know: hang around, see how easy the place was to get into. From what he said when he phoned in this afternoon, it seems he wasn't the only one hanging around. All coming and going pretty freely. Some pretty rough types, too. These guards the kids saw—they seem to be there to keep a sharp eye on the machinery and supplies but don't pay much attention to their visitors."

The children nodded and settled in for what promised to be a long tale.

"It turned out to be a good idea sending Jamieson. This afternoon Tom Kibben—you know him, Owen? Smooth, gray-haired, just about lives at the Country Club? Anyway, he dropped by to see me. Seems he does a bit of legal work for Minshew Coal from time to time, whenever Minshew needs a man in Kennington."

"But what did he *say?*" Arthur burst out.

Mr. Arthur laughed. "Hold your horses, Arthur. Rob here can't tell a story without a good long build-up. He'll get to the point in his own good time."

Mr. Padgett grinned. "But will the audience survive, eh? Well, in effect, what he said was that my 'rumor' had come to Minshew. The proverbial little bird had told him, I suppose. Kibben suggested that I might do well to tread easy. Nobody had seen young Stephen here land in the drink except the children, and as he put it, 'You know kids and their stories.' Said that trespassers were kept out, that the place was well guarded. In fact, he claimed the guard had seen them out and down the road."

"He never did!" Miggle sputtered. "That's not true."

"I know, I know!" Mr. Padgett threw up his hands in mock defense. "That's why it's a good thing I had young Jamieson out here," he explained. "At about two o'clock or so—same time Tom Kibben was with me—the guards cleared all the hangers-on out. They must have had the word on a two-way radio the foreman has up there."

Mr. Arthur nodded. "They run quite a show up there. We can see something of it from the boys' room. We'll go up and give you a look at it before you go."

The lawyer was astonished to hear that the great machines worked twenty-four hours a day.

"I suppose Minshew figures it's so much less time for any real opposition to shape up," snorted Mr. Arthur. "If he can rip the mountain up in one year instead of two, he may beat these new laws we're working for. The Governor knows that nine out of ten of these strip-mining outfits are delighted to pay a fine of a few hundred dollars. That's a drop in the bucket compared to what it would cost them to fill in and replant their diggings."

Turning to Arthur, Mr. Arthur said, "I trimmed our letter down a bit and had it telegraphed to the Capitol first thing this morning. The Governor is really pushing this thing. I had a phone call this afternoon from a member of a new fact-finding commission he's set up. Thanked us for the information and said he'd keep in touch. Some of those coal operators have literally been pushing people out of their homes with bulldozers. They're careful with the more prosperous farmers like Barhatch and town folk like us, but they thought it was safe enough to push the poorer folks around. That was just down in Deer Lick Hollow. Anyway, it looks as if we'll be getting some action at last."

The children exchanged glances. "At last" might be too late.

Mrs. Arthur came in with a pot of hot chocolate and a fresh pot of coffee. She filled cups all around.

"Mr. Padgett," said Arthur. "Did the man from your office stay out here after—oh, say three o'clock?"

"Yes." The lawyer looked up quizzically from his coffee cup. "Funny thing, that. Have you heard about the accident they had?"

"No. What?" Trish and Kit, who had come in for hot chocolate, pricked up their ears at this and sat down on the floor beside Miggle to listen.

With such an attentive audience Mr. Padgett spun a dramatic tale. Mr. Jamieson had found a tree-shaded rock on the hillside above the Bane and settled down to see just how Minshew Coal Company operated. At about half past three there was an odd rumble that seemed to come from a deep ravine on the downhill side—where he supposed the lake must be. Dust began to swirl. Almost immediately, one of the great drag-line machines, moving along a wide shelf directly above the growing cloud of dust, began to slide sideways down the slope. Slowly, as if in a slow-motion film, it overbalanced and toppled into the ravine, its great mouth clanging open and shut. In the confusion that followed, it had not been difficult to reenter the diggings. Some brave soul had snared the driver of the machine out of the seething water with a crowbar. No one else would approach the dusty pit where occasional small landslides cascaded into the roiling waters. The cry of "earthquake" went up, and workmen headed for the road. Jamieson had, to his amazement, seen them turned back to their machines by the armed guards. He wisely made his own exit, unseen, up a narrow gully into the Wood. The dust eventually subsided and work took up again, but sullenly, and only in the reaches of the Bane that were furthest from Banebottom.

Mr. Padgett was repeating Mr. Jamieson's comments on the low quality of the coal being trucked out of the Bane when the telephone rang. Mrs. Arthur went to answer it. The others could hear her talking excitedly, and after a few moments she came into the living room and beckoned to Arthur.

"It's your father, calling from Poole. He wants to talk to you."

Torn between the long-distance telephone call and the talk of the Bane, Arthur left the room reluctantly and then dashed down the hall to the library phone.

* * *

"The stuff isn't suitable for industrial use," Mr. Padgett continued. "Apparently, it goes to the county school system. And they have to take it, whether or no. As I understand it, years ago, when other fuels began to threaten the market in coal, some of the local coal mine operators had the foresight to have the county enter into an agreement that the schools would use coal as long as it was offered to them. The county—understandably—wanted to support a local industry; and coal *was* cheaper. But now schools that want to switch to gas or oil heating because it's cleaner and more efficient *and* not so hard on the school custodian's back are stuck with coal as long as someone like Minshew wants to unload it on them . . ."

Arthur returned, a stricken look on his face, to interrupt.

"Yes? What is it, Arthur?" asked his uncle.

"Dad wants to talk to you for a minute, Uncle Owen."

Then, as his uncle went to the telephone, Arthur went out the front door and down the porch steps to stand in the dark garden.

"What is it? What's the matter?" asked Miggle. She and the others had slipped out after him.

"Everything." His voice caught. "You see, Dad's going to this big conference in San Francisco. He's been planning on it for a long time. He was going to fly out next week. But now he and Mom have decided to drive out so she and I can see California, and I'm supposed to take the bus home from Kennington tomorrow night. We leave Wednesday morning."

"But—what will we do if you go?" Stevie whispered the question for all of them.

"You–you'll be O.K. But *I* won't be." He swallowed. "When I said I didn't want to go, Dad got mad. I guess I don't blame him. It was mostly for me they decided to drive all that way. So what could I do but say it was all right? They wanted me to catch the morning bus that comes from Kittamaugy and goes by way of Colwyn, but I stalled; so they said the night one would be O.K. if I didn't mind stepping out of the bus and starting for California an hour later."

"Oh, crumbs! Oh, double spit!" groaned Miggle.

The night-blooming jasmine blew sweetly about them. The great floodlamps glared through the hilltop trees, but the Elephants were silent. That silence, so long hoped for, was now ominous and frightening. Time was short for more reasons than one.

Chapter Twenty

Morning slipped into the valley under that same silence. Breakfast was a glum affair, and the children went about their chores with the animals slowly and not in the best of tempers. Miggle stepped on an egg some thoughtless hen had laid on the coop floor where she could not miss it as she came in the door. It was not a very large egg, but it was the last straw. She roared around the room flapping her arms, throwing their breakfast of cracked grain in the air, and making a horrid noise. Chickens pedaled wildly in the air, squawking out of her way.

"There! See if I care if you don't lay any eggs for a week!" She slammed the door.

Happily, the grim beginning to the day did not last. Shortly before nine o'clock the silence on the mountain was broken by the cough and rumble of diesel motors starting up. There was none of the creaking and squealing of cables, which the Elephants made at their digging, but some business was afoot. Suddenly, between house and chicken coop and barn, buckets and pitchforks and currycombs flew at double time. If there was something afoot, the sooner they reached the woods behind Hazel Baker's barn the better.

An hour later at the window over the Wood, the children saw the busy scurrying of bulldozers in the Bane. The two remaining Elephants were also now at work.

"There has been a watcher at the window since we parted yester evening," Durwen explained. "When Eirin, in the first hour past dawn, saw a long black motorcar creep up the road and turn into the Bane, our curiosity was roused. Illurin and Nirin were sent to watch from some closer place, as we can see little from here but the entrance and the further reaches. Nirin still watches, but Illurin returned only a few moments before your coming. What they have seen is most curious."

Leaving Meruel by the window, they slipped behind the heavy curtain into the central chamber. There Illurin and several others waited with Maelin.

"It is the man Minshew in the car," continued Durwen. "He sits there yet, with the glass windows fast closed and a guard nearby."

Illurin took up the tale. The children were held speechless.

"He must have found the night workers idling, for he was berating them roundly as we crept close. There was a laurel thicket near their tool shed which gave us shelter. There was much talk. At last, when he could neither persuade nor frighten them back to use the long-necked machines to pull the sunken machine from the water, he blustered that their talk of earthquakes was nonsense. *He* would go take a look! The water could be no more than fifteen feet deep, and the machine *must* be salvaged. The lake must be filled in, but not until the expensive machine was safely out. The workers shouted warnings after the car as it moved down into the Bane. The driver was hunched over the wheel—I think he had been shaken by the tales of the men."

The company heard how, with Nirin, Illurin raced to the lower eastern rim. There was at the edge of the Wood a tall tree that afforded a clear sight down onto road and lake. High in its stout branches they had been screened from view. The pit still lay in dusk, for daylight had not yet reached so deep. The lake, to their left, was quiet. Pebbles and small cascades of loose earth still slid beneath the dark surface, but the endless sucking had stopped. The lake had been choked by its own greed. Of the machine only the great jaws were to be seen, hanging by their cables at the top of the long neck. They hung open, and the evil of the place made it seem as if they were caught in some wordless cry of protest. The black car slowed and stopped well up the road, and a heavy figure—Mr. Minshew—heaved himself out of the back seat. He stood staring in the road and then began slowly to walk toward the water, drawn by a dreadful curiosity. His violent manner and purposeful movement were strangely subdued. Perhaps he was dazed at the thought of the money lost; perhaps by the puzzle of the hole which could swallow a steel monster over a hundred feet long from its base to the tip of its boom. Fists clenched, he stopped. The water had begun to stir, not violently as before, but slowly, as if there were some deep pulse in it. Then, helpless, Illurin and Nirin had seen the fat man jerk and begin to

totter forward. He ran like a man who is about to fall at every step, blindly, his hands thrown wide in protest, toward the water.

"We could not have helped." Illurin shuddered. "If the

driver of the car had not overcome his fear and run to stop his master, the water would have claimed him."

"The evil under the hill is angry indeed when it would devour its own," said Durwen. "Yet good can come when evil bares itself too rashly. Illurin tells us that Minshew ordered the pushing machines with great blades . . ."

"Bulldozers."

"Ah, bulldozers. He set them to work filling in the lower road and piling up a barrier for the long-necks to work behind. From this safety they have been heaping earth into Banebottom and the deeper cuts with great industry while the bulldozers scurry about, scraping and leveling." He fingered the key, which hung on his breast on a fine chain of the same metal.

Illurin laughed. "Though all could see how pale and shaken this Minshew was, he would not admit before the men that there was anything of terror in the place. When he gave the orders to fill it in, he blustered that—how was it?—that 'the state was on his tail and he couldn't afford to be sued for drowning kiddies.' There would be time enough to get at the deepest coal when the 'fuss' had died down."

"The deepest coal?" Miggle frowned. "That's down toward us, isn't it?"

Arthur said, "He might be greedy enough to try again if he could get anybody to dig at it. If we—if you could use the water to keep them away for a while, the Governor and Uncle Owen and the farmers would have time to stop it." He explained his uncle's news to the folk, who sat on cushions on the grass-strewn floor as the children did.

"Ah, so!" breathed Túdual, coming forward with Rhelemon from the book-lined niche where they had been sitting. "So the Nameless One will be bound indeed!"

Rhelemon moved to touch Arthur lightly upon the shoulder. "Yet you ask only that we turn the waters 'for a while.' Why is that?"

He avoided her eyes.

"Because then the mountain will be safe. Won't it?"

"Safe? Yes. The Nameless Thing would return to its long sleep. Come, say what it is you would have us do with the waters afterwards. Shall we then turn them from the hill and Wood? Shall we leave dry the bared bones of the mountain so that twice a hundred years must turn before the wound is healed?"

Arthur looked first to Miggle and then to the other children. They nodded. Miggle's eyes were stars.

"Yes," he said firmly. "You can turn the waters west and ride the flood out to the rivers and the sea. You can finish going home."

The suspense of the company burst like a clear bubble that scatters a fresh and sparkling mist. They smiled and spoke in floods of words. The room shimmered with dim light. Maelin reached wide her arms to the children.

"A free gift freely given! And the gift, though you may have doubted it, was in your giving alone, for the key was of your finding." She took Miggle's hand in hers.

Rhelemon smiled. "We have kept faith with men, though they have blamed us in many matters in order to free themselves from blame. Your hearts listen more wisely. And I would not have us regard this gift lightly despite the speech Durwen frets to make to you." She held up a hand to her daughter's lord. "I would have Garym tell them what he has told us of what the waters mean to the Bane. They must know how much the gift *could* cost."

Garym spoke softly, weaving pictures with his words.

Now that the deep reaches of the Bane were being filled, if the six welling springs and the falling stream were freed upon the Bane, the ugly land could be made to bear and blossom once again. The thirsty ground would drink the water. Drying springs on the slope below would once more rise and flow. The first outfall into the Run would be a bitter draught indeed; but once all was washed clean, fish would sport in its pools. The crumbling earth, too wet in its deeps to allow digging, could yet be shifted and smoothed to make hillocks and meadows. Seedlings of the trembling aspen would take root quickly and grow to shelter shrubs and trees that would by themselves falter and die in such harsh soil. The children could–after not so many years–bring their own children to pick wild raspberries in the clearings and listen to the white-throated sparrow's song.

Miggle grew sadder and sadder as he went on. Her lovely mountain, come back as fair as before. It was very hard.

Garym finished. He kept his calm gaze fast upon the children.

"That–that would be nice," Miggle faltered, brushing a strand of blond hair from her eyes. "But still, we'd rather you went. Who knows what might happen if you waited here for the Bane to bloom? I mean, the river might dry up or go some other way than under the Great Hall and down. Things like that do happen, don't they? Anything might happen."

Rhelemon nodded. "There is love indeed; and we accept it with like love. You must not think hardly of us for seeming to test you harshly. We are too used to the betrayals of men. But now we may speak openly. There *is* a way in which we may have our freedom and yet give you back your Wood as it was."

Stevie leaned forward. He had sensed from the first that in the warmth and welcome that surrounded them something good was hidden, waiting.

Durwen spoke carefully. "Do not leap too soon! It is a way which means toil and no little risk for you."

"We don't care about that! What is it?" Stevie and Arthur answered together.

"Our thought was this: if our company set sail from the jeweled caverns below the long falls, riding out into the world upon the flood, your maps—" Here he smiled briefly as Káolin grinned at Miggle's accusing glance. "Your maps tell us that the journey to the first of the rivers would take perhaps an hour. Our boats are swift. When we were in deeping waters and past the need of Nũtayẽ's flood, you children could turn its clear rush upon the Bane. There would be dangers. The one—or ones—whom we call Nameless would be waking yet, and its power to daunt men's minds is great. And even if your strength be sufficient in that, we must set a word of closing upon the gates of Nũtayẽ. By opening those of east and west, we have the three gates of the song; and by then closing the western and the threshold gates we are left with 'seven the gates and one the door,' that one being the stream above the Bane. It makes good sense to close the city. Men must never find their way here.

"The western portal would shut itself against all seekers once the flood had ceased, and the threshold, which is your way to us, would be set to close at the hour when you were likely free of it. It would pass from men's sight forever. Time would be scarce. Were you delayed and trapped here, it would be a woeful thing."

They protested. "We wouldn't be. We can do it."

"But the key?" Miggle wondered. "What about the key?"

Maelin looked at her gravely. "It would be yours again —more a burden than a treasure, I fear. We would have no need of it in Tir na'nOg. It is a thing of this earth between the two worlds, and it must stay here."

"Why do you say a 'burden'?" Miggle asked.

"Because we know not to what other uses such a thing might be put. It must be hidden wisely and guarded well. Those who joy in wielding power might find other evils to loose with it."

"Oh." Miggle rubbed her hands together nervously.

Despite the worry and warnings of the Fair Folk, the children held firm. It was Kit, her freckles drawn together in a frown, who threw everything into confusion. She and Trish were restless at so much talk.

"When are you going, then? Arthur has to go home tonight. Will he have to miss it all?"

They had forgotten. Arthur himself had forgotten. Miserable, they explained.

"Where then is your home?" asked Durwen.

"Poole. That's in Ohio."

"The names mean little to us. How many leagues is it from us here?"

"About a hundred miles. By Highway 32, that is. The way the old Kennington bus goes, you'd think it was four hundred. It doesn't get in until after six in the morning."

"Where are the maps?" Durwen signed to Enniaun, who brought them from a bench in one of the grottoes. They were still in the old paper sack.

"Show me here." Durwen spread a tattered map across his knees.

"Umm . . . there." Arthur indicated a black dot beside the blue line of the Ohio River.

"And we are here." Durwen laid a thoughtful finger along the Ridge. Then he said, "These markings across the rivers I take to be bridges. They are clearly roads springing from one bank to another. But what of these?" He pointed to several faint single lines that spanned the Ohio. "What are they?"

Arthur puzzled at the locations while Stevie and the others craned to look.

"Those must be the spillways where the river level falls. There are locks over along the east bank here. Barges and paddleboats go into the locks, you see; and then the water level is let down, and they steam out at the end of the lock below the falls."

Durwen frowned. "These are the things we know too little of. Our boats are light and easily carried, so we need no 'locks'; but must we make portage at night through the streets of men? Where can we shelter through the day? There seem to be so many villages and towns."

"There are the islands," said Arthur. "Lots of them, once you reach the Ohio. People have vegetable gardens out on some of the big ones, but lots are so narrow or little that nobody bothers with them. They've got trees from stem to stern. They run right down to the water and trail their branches in it." He looked up excitedly. "There's one out from our house that Stevie and Mig have been on. We used to have a tree house out there. They're good places for holing up."

Durwen traced the waterway: Lickpiddy, Monongahela, Ohio; after them the great wide river to the sea and then eastward to the ocean. His finger paused over the locks and lingered among the islands as he calculated time and speed. Slowly, he folded the map. He looked at his folk and their elders searchingly.

"Why should we not go tonight? And the boy with us as far as his island and his home?"

Chapter Twenty-One

Miggle sat in the window seat in the loft bedroom, her feet tucked under her. Stevie nodded in an armchair. Both wore bathrobes but underneath were still fully dressed. Kit and Trish dozed on the big double bed. The younger girls had been doubtful when Miggle asked them whether they would go to Nũtayẽ after dark. They had been frightened by the fogs of the Bane, and the heavy beating anger that had pressed into the cavern of the waterways had confused and dismayed them, but these things had soon been forgotten. No, it wasn't that. And certainly they had spent an enchanted morning in the bowers of Nũtayẽ while the folk sorted through chests and storerooms dividing what must be left behind from those things that would be needed on the journey. Among the things to be left behind there had been many garments, plain but brightly colored; strands of tiny cave pearls; eggshell-thin cups and bowls carved from jade or rose quartz or stone that glowed like gold against the light; goblets, dishes, and flagons of *findruin* or the dull silver-like metal, all of which had been brought long ago from Coed y Dugoed Mawr. The girls had helped in the work. Not to go back to say good-by? It wasn't quite that. Periel, Meruel, and Alianor had already given them "going-away presents"—ribbons, a fragile crystal butterfly, a flower carved of jade. They had said good-by already. They would wait up for Miggle and Stevie if they had to, but they didn't *have* to go, did they?

Miggle was perplexed. *She* could not have been kept away from Nũtayẽ by anything short of a strait jacket. How *could* Trisha and Kit go on so about her mother's offer to spend tomorrow morning teaching them how to make and glaze their own pottery beads for necklaces? As if one last look at Nũtayẽ wasn't worth all the pottery beads made and unmade now and the year after tomorrow! She rubbed her chin on her drawn-up knees. The sillies had not been fifteen minutes in falling asleep.

Arthur had gotten off all right. The last bus to Kennington stopped at five forty-five at the corner of the road from Tipple—just past the Bakers' barn. It had been easy for Arthur and his suitcase to disappear into the Wood while his cousins walked on to the Tipple road. They had waited for the bus to pass and then turned home. Mr. Arthur arrived home half an hour later. He asked whether Arthur had gotten off all right, whether Mrs. Arthur had telephoned Kennington to reserve him a seat on the night bus, whether he had enough money for his supper in the coach station and for something to read until time to board the bus at nine o'clock. The children's vague yeses were truthful, if misleading. Mrs. Arthur had telephoned, reserving a bus seat next to a window and, being concerned about the long wait between buses, had thought of arranging for Arthur to have dinner with the Padgetts. Arthur had looked so distressed at the idea that she decided she was being over-fussy. He was certainly old enough to order a decent dinner and get on the right bus. "He was really very excited about going when the time came," she reported to Mr. Arthur, smiling. "I expect California was too much to resist."

Miggle tiptoed across the room to peer at the clock on the bedstand. It was already past ten. Her parents could be heard moving quietly about their room as they prepared to turn in early. There were no lights in the orchard yet. She returned to her watching, arms around her legs, chin on her knees.

They came at last: lights moving like fireflies under the trees, wavering downward, clustering beneath the willow and locust trees on the hillside between the spring and barnyard. One figure separated from the shadows, coming silently to the house and up the narrow steps to the landing outside the window. It was Arthur. He tapped lightly and signed for Miggle to open the middle window. It had been closed and the windows at each side left open and screened so that they would not need to struggle with its ratcheting stubborn screen, waking the whole house. Miggle turned the handle on the middle window, opening it outward. Arthur's eyes gleamed with excitement and moonlight.

"Hurry up! Give Stevie a nudge. Trisha and Kit aren't coming, are they?"

Miggle had turned to waken Stevie.

Káolin joined Arthur outside the window.

"Are the small ones to come?" he asked doubtfully.

"Maelin set Periel and the others to discourage their coming. It would not be wise. The stair from the Window Hall to the waterways is long and arduous, and that from the waterways down past the long falls more difficult yet."

Miggle whispered in answer, "The sillies don't want to come. They said they'd wait up, but I bet they don't."

She moved to the bed and jiggled the mattress, but the girls scarcely stirred. She shrugged and slipped out of her robe. Already Stevie was clambering over the window seat and out onto the landing. The flashlight hanging on his Scout belt clanged against the window. Miggle pulled one side curtain shut, putting the night light between it and the window. Then she followed, and the three children and Káolin tiptoed down the stairway to the garden. The window was left open and the watchers sleeping. Willy, who had been left loose for the night, followed after them.

In the chamber where the waterways divided, Miggle and Stevie peered back up the narrow stair. Its lamps flickered away upward into dimness. It thrust downward to this point from the Window Hall above, a straight shaft piercing solid rock, but not a steep one. The steps were wide and low, the sort that are awkward and difficult to hurry on because they are too wide to take one at a time. Where the other stairs and passageways of Nũtayẽ followed ancient stream beds or natural passages, winding and curving, this one had been carved by skillful hands out of living rock. How long ago it had been made, no one could guess. Stevie rubbed his knees and–still bent over –moved them back and forth, bending and locking them. Miggle simply leaned over, putting her weight through her hands onto her knees, stretching the muscles up the backs of her legs.

"That's a lot of stairs," said Arthur, to be saying something. Everyone was so quiet.

"*You* won't have to run all the way back up them," snorted Stevie.

"Look, you two." Miggle watched as Durwen took the key from around his neck and inserted it in the sea-star mark in the wall. The air, she thought, was so thick that every movement seemed to take forever.

The folk who had gone with Arthur to fetch Miggle and Stevie warned the children to stand well clear. They stepped back against the wall, where Káolin and Eirin made room for them.

Durwen turned the key twice, full around. The heavy tongue of rock rumbled forward, thrusting under the water. The water roared and swirled, frothing down through the second hole until it, too, was blocked by the great stone slab. Immediately, the water swept around the curve of the ancient channel, hissing over dry sand and rolling on. Where it disappeared through the archway set in the western–the right–wall of the chamber, the channel ran some ten or fifteen yards and stopped, sending the water over its edge to a floor a hundred feet below. There, after a moment, the listeners could hear it crash and run roaring on to fall again and then again.

"The great falls are four," said Durwen. "And our way goes by their side. Come. There is no time to waste."

Through the archway a narrow path followed the river's edge. At the rim of the falls this passageway opened out near the roof of a great long chamber, dimly lit. The water leaped out and fell, a veil of foam, to the floor far below.

There it gathered itself out of the noise and spray to flow out of sight under a low vaulted roof. The stair was cut in the rock wall. It was steep and came to an end at the lower floor level well this side of the place where the river vanished under its vault.

Arthur and Stevie looked over the edge unperturbed, but Miggle shrank back against the wall. She saw no rail. Her knees felt like water. She wanted horribly to say, "Please, can't I stay here? Stevie can climb back up to say when you've gotten away safe." She wanted to say it, but she was too ashamed. Once she had gotten halfway up a spiral staircase that had no railing or pole in the center and had frozen there, terrified. It was on a school field trip to the old stone fort at Wissburg. She had backed all the way down, trembling, and gone to sit in the school bus, where she washed her streaky face and dirty knees with a handkerchief and spit. She had never told anybody.

She was torn. This was different. If she didn't tell now, she might get everybody stuck on the narrow stair. Or she might never get back up without somebody both behind and before. When it happened, her knees wouldn't listen to her head, no matter what. She didn't have to be scared even. It was awful.

Káolin looked at her questioningly. "Come, we are last. I will follow you."

Running her hand along the wall, she shuffled her feet forward rather than picking them up and putting them down normally. She kept her eyes averted from the falls. The water pulled your eyes to the edge and pulled you with them. Her nose started to run. She sniffled. She had a handkerchief but was afraid to put her hand in her pocket. Her *dumb* nose.

Káolin's sure fingers took her right hand and closed it around a stout rope. Startled, she saw that the rope stretched from a heavy iron ring by the top stair, where she stood, through similar rings set about every ten feet down the length of the stair. Above each ring a niche cut into the wall held a flaring lamp.

"Oh, that's better," she exclaimed. Gradually, she caught up to the line of downward-moving figures. It was easy so long as she remembered at each of the rings to hold on with her left hand as her right left the rope to take hold again past the ring. Ahead, only Dub and Stevie were using the rope. Stevie's hand ran along it lightly.

From the bottom of the stair the children were led beside the river into the next chamber. There, too, were falls and a stair. The chamber itself was fairer even than the last. Both floor and ceiling were uneven, crowded with pinnacles and pendants of many colors, which forested the banks of the stream. The stair—at times a sloping path without steps—wound down among the pinnacles and columns. At their bases masses of pale crystal flowers bloomed. The way was easy, and Durwen, at the head of the company, hurried. Miggle would have lingered if Káolin had not been behind her. The thought of how much would be lost when Nũtayẽ was sealed up forever came upon her like a dark shadow. Her eyes stung, and she stumbled.

Stevie was wondering at the idea of a lost Nũtayẽ, too. How queer to think that it would go on and on, growing crystal flowers in the dark forever. Were things beautiful when there was nobody to see them? He touched a white blossom growing from a crevice in a pillar, and under his fingers it crumbled to a fine powder that swirled in the air as he passed. He put his hands in his pockets.

The third stair was long and steep like the first. Beside it the falls fell in long steps, a wide cascade like white lace. It filled the air with mist, and the lamps along the wall were haloed with gold. The ceiling and walls seemed wreathed with twining leafy creepers, all stone–gold and green and red.

The fourth stair again was easier, and at its foot the larger part of the folk waited. There were more torches and lamps here, for the walls were darker and the darkness heavier. The water ran swiftly past and into the shadows, sliding under the hill to the western gate.

The four boats bobbed and strained against their moorings in the swift water. In the middle of each coracle a small chest had been stowed. Brackets were fastened around the sides of these, and the broad paddles were fixed there, standing straight up like a crown of feathers amidships. On the shore, shadowy in the light of smoky torches and the winking lamps, the companies gathered and divided. The folk seemed now, as they had at the very first, oddly alike. Red-gold hair and silvered eyes gleamed in the lamplight. Each wore a long cloak, gray until with some movement it flickered pale rose or green, blue or fawn—the same silken colors cunningly hidden in pigeon feathers.

Miggle fingered the cloak that had been put around Arthur's shoulders. It was soft as a pigeon's breast and beautiful. In it Dub looked different, dark and pale: "Arthur," not "Dub."

Stevie and Miggle went with him to the first boat. Eirin

and Illurin drew it close under the bank, and Durwen stepped after Rhelemon and Maelin into the bow. He signed for Arthur to follow. Túdual, Garym, and Káolin led into the three remaining boats, each taking the high place in the prow.

Rhelemon was nearest to the shore of those in the first boat. She reached out to touch a light finger against Stevie's forehead and Miggle's hand.

"Do not grieve, my dears. You are setting the caged birds free."

"I wish we could come, too," Stevie whispered.

Rhelemon smiled at him. "Perhaps if any mortal could find the way, it would be one who lived a moment as deeply as you do. But it is impossible; and we will pass with that moment. You will move on to tomorrow. That is as it should be."

She took a small object from Maelin's hand and laid it in Stevie's palm. It was the carven treelike piece from the *fidchell* game, which there had been no time to learn. To Miggle she handed the gleaming key on its bright chain. Miggle hung it around her neck as Durwen had carried it. She blinked and had to pull out her handkerchief and blow her nose.

"Come," said Rhelemon, touching her cheek. "You cannot hold a tadpole forever in a cup or wish leaves green in the red autumn or forbid a snowflake to melt. There is nothing—neither beauty nor sorrow—in this middle world which does not pass. Even we are only shadows of what we were. And the faster you hold to the flower, the faster it fades; the caged bird pines and its feathers fall; the new-hatched robin and the gardenia bloom will die from your

touch. Oh, child!" She shook her head. "Beauty is not in the having but the being; not alone in the sight but in the seeing. A blade of grass is as beautiful as all Nũtayẽ . . . until you pluck it."

Miggle looked up, nodding. "I know. That's what Dub

–Arthur is always telling me. I like to put things in boxes, he says. I *do* try to remember not to–really I do."

Arthur reddened, and everyone smiled at them. The boats strained to be free.

Durwen said to Miggle, "One thing you may keep fast

in a box forever, and good fortune attend the keeping." He pointed to the key upon her breast. "Nũtayẽ will be lost, yet who knows what other locks Argána's key may fit? Remember: by the time you reach the top of the fourth stair, we will be safe in deeping waters. Do not wait. Turn the key in its lock one turn back and no more. Stay only to see that the water flows aright. There is ample time for you to climb the straight stair to the Window Hall. The dog watches for you there, I think?"

"Yes, sir." Arthur nodded. "We told him to stay there."

"Very well. Remember," he warned Stevie and Miggle, "let nothing delay you on the stairs or in the chambers above. These lamps will burn for several hours yet, but do not tarry to marvel at sights along the way. The last gate of Nũtayẽ will close, leaving you to watch the lamps flicker out one by one into sullen darkness, if you do."

He turned to the boats behind. "Come! We go. Cast loose and follow!"

"I'll write a letter first thing tomorrow," Arthur called. His voice already sounded distant and unreal.

Miggle and Stevie watched as the coracles began to move. The paddles were lifted free and flashed out to ripple the water as the boats whipped away. The streaming torches smoked and flared and threw tall shadows on the walls. A sound of singing came back across the water. As the cavern narrowed over the river, the torches were extinguished.

"Take care!" Káolin's voice sang out from the last boat. "Farewell!"

They were alone beneath the mountain.

Epilogue

Midnight

Stevie had pushed Miggle up the last flight of steps—the wide stair from the Hall of the Column to the threshold of Nũtayẽ. Neither of them had known what it was like to be so tired. So many steps. Miggle had mumbled over and over, "I just want to lie down. I don't *care* if I never get up again." But Stevie caught at her each time and pushed her ahead. His own knees seemed as if they would start bending backwards at any moment, but the words, "The last gate will close," echoed in his ears. He pushed and threatened and pinched, until together they sat upon the grass in the laurel-ringed meadow outside the tumble-down rock house that was the threshold of Nũtayẽ.

Miggle stretched out on the ground beneath the stars and drew deep breaths. Fresh air. It was like sweet apple wine after the closeness that had closed around her and clung to her from the moment she had touched Argána's key to the lock by the stream. Either her imagination or a voice that spoke through that dead air kept saying, "See! What power you have! Come, do not be foolish. Keep the city for your own. Make haste to the threshold. You need only drop a feather—a blue stone or a feather—in the gateway as you go, and you may come back at will." Somehow she had closed her ears. She felt for the feather ribbon around her waist, and it was still there. The key hung on its chain. She slipped it inside her shirt.

"Mig! Look!" Stevie's whisper held amazement. Willy barked.

Miggle sat up, brushing damp strands of hair from her eyes.

The gate of the threshold had closed. While they watched, the stones that had seemed a house of sorts wavered, grew transparent, and slowly faded. There was nothing there but the sheer rock wall, rising out of grass and weeds against a dark sky.

The grass was damp. Willy whined to go home.

Middle-night

Miggle awoke with a start, her hand upon the key. Her eyes strained at the dark. Kit and Trish were as motionless in the big bed in the corner as they had been on her return. They had wakened at some time and, forgetting their watch, had crept back to their own bed.

They had not moved, and the world outside was heavy with sleep. Why had she awakened? She had—yes, she had been dreaming. She tried to remember whose voice she had heard. Maelin's? Yes, Maelin. "It must be hidden wisely and guarded well . . . other evils to loose . . ."

But she wasn't always as wise as she should be; and in

the dream she had seen herself forgetting. She had seen her own blank eyes as Dub said, "You remember: in Nũtayẽ . . ." Then, too, boxes were made to be opened.

She stared at the dark rectangle of the window in the darker wall. The vase of roses on the small table beside the window caught the light from the headlamps of a passing car. Hazel Baker's big brother, probably.

Miggle pushed the covers back and sat up. She groped for her slippers and took the flashlight from the bed-table drawer. Quietly, stepping near the wall and well away from the centers of the stair treads, she made her way downstairs, into the kitchen, and down the cellar steps.

She looked in the peephole of the kiln at the carefully stacked vases. The kiln was just beginning really to glow. The heat had to build up very slowly. The thermostat read 900°. Miggle knew that what she was going to do might crack the whole batch of pottery, but if she was very quick, it would be all right. Unfastening the key from its chain, she held it with a pair of long wooden-handled tongs. She undid the catch on the kiln door. Taking a deep breath, she pulled the door open only far enough to thrust the tongs in and drop the key into the nearest pot. Quickly, she closed the door and fastened it. The thermostat sank to 500° and held there. There was at least no sound of cracking. The thermostat began once more its slow edging upward. Miggle hoped *findruin* would melt. It might make the vase a funny shape, but she could keep flowers in it, anyway.

She yawned widely and, switching on the flashlight for a moment, found the stairs and headed back to bed.

Arthur's feet were wet. He stood on the back porch looking down at them. "I should've worn my tennis shoes," he said to himself. He set the suitcase down carefully, quietly, and peered through one of the narrow windows beside the door.

His mother moved about the brightly lit kitchen in her dressing gown, filling Thermos jugs and making sandwiches. He raised his hand to knock on the door frame, hesitated, then turned quickly to slip down the steps and race back through the dawn-pale side yard, avoiding the yellow-green pools of light that spilled over the grass from the waking house.

Across the gray street and through the morning twilight in the lilac bushes, he came to the fence and the gate at the cliff top. The river stretched past below, wide and silver. Midway out from the hill-high bank to the further shore, the island held dusk fast beneath its thick canopy of trees. Dub leaned on the fence and strained to see beneath the branches that trailed in the distant water. The four small boats were nowhere to be seen. He hadn't really expected to see them. Even when he stood on the tiny dock at the foot of the stair saying good-by, the pigeon-feathered cloaks had shimmered like the river in the dawn. From a few feet away the coracles had been unclear, indistinct.

He looked down to the landing directly below, where his dad's rowboat swung on its tether. Something green lay on the planks of the landing. Opening the gate, Dub clattered down the rickety wooden stair.

It was a blackened wooden box about six inches square and three inches deep, wrapped in a length of green cloth.

Sitting on the bottom step, Dub read the note pinned to the cloth: "There is no skill in the Middle World to unwind the secrets written here of Nũtayẽ. We have tried to unlock the letters, but to no avail. Yet the book itself is beautiful, and yours. The last in believing shall be longest in forgetting."

The book inside had for covers polished plaques of the rose crystal of Nũtayẽ, and the clasp was like pale gold. The pages were covered with closely written signs in many colors. Arthur returned it to the box and, wrapping the cloth securely around it, put it under his arm and climbed back up to the gate. Across the street the new sun flared in the windows of the houses.

"Someday I *will* read it," he said to himself.

His mother came to the back door.

"Arthur! What are you doing *here?*" She turned to look at the clock. "Your bus isn't due for an hour yet. We haven't packed the car."

He carried his suitcase into the kitchen.

"I got a ride with some friends," he said. "What's for breakfast?"

And After

The Bane grew green. The Arthurs' spring overflowed even in the drought of August. And the folk came at last to Tir na'nOg.